quick bright things

*stories
by
ron
wallace*

MID-LIST PRESS
FIRST SERIES: SHORT FICTION

Copyright © 1988, 1989, 1990, 1991, 1992, 1993, 1994, 1995, 1996, 1997, 2000 by Ron Wallace. All rights reserved. No part of this book may be used or reproduced in any manner whatsoever without permission in writing from the publisher, except by a reviewer who may quote brief passages in a review.

Published by Mid-List Press, 4324 12th Avenue South, Minneapolis, MN 55407; www.midlist.org.

First printing: February 2000
04 03 02 01 00   5 4 3 2 1

Manufactured in the United States of America

Library of Congress Cataloging-in-Publication Data
  Wallace, Ronald.
      Quick bright things : stories / by Ron Wallace.
         p. cm.
      "First series--short fiction."
      ISBN 0-922811-44-X (alk. paper)
      1. Family--United States--Fiction. 2. Domestic fiction, American. I. Title.
  PS3573.A4314 Q54 2000
  813'.54--dc21   99-088117

Cover and text design: Lane Stiles
*Cover illustration: **Young Corn**.* Grant Wood, 1931. Oil on masonite panel, 23 1/2 x 29 7/8 inches. Copyright © Cedar Rapids, Iowa, Community School District. Memorial to Linnie Schloeman, Woodrow Wilson School.

This is a work of fiction. Names, characters, places, and incidents are either the product of the author's imagination or are used fictitiously, and any resemblance to actual persons, living or dead, events, or locales is entirely coincidental.

quick
bright
things

for my family

contents

talking	1
the little woman	13
the night nurse	21
wordplay	26
the quarry	36
men at work	50
cross country	52
skin	66
a trick of memory	68
yogurt	82
the new sidewalks	84
the sacred well	92
no answer	105
logjam	107
jackknife	116
animal rights	118
wrestling	134
siding	136
worry	138
topless in tucson	140
quick bright things	157

"So quick bright things come to confusion."
—*A Midsummer Night's Dream*

talking

1"Is there something you want to talk about?" my father said.

He was propped up in the old mahogany four-poster bed in my grandmother's back bedroom. It was a room that was rarely used, at the end of a crooked corridor in her dark Victorian house. The lavender flowered wallpaper was peeling off the walls like huge scabs; the floor was mottled, and rough as a cough; the dirty manila-colored shades were drawn, their soiled ring pulls dangling in the dim light.

He was staring at me expectantly, as if I'd done something wrong and should confess. But I was less afraid than irritated.

"No," I said.

He set his mouth and looked away. We had come to my grandmother's house in Elm Grove, Iowa, the house in which my father grew up, at the beginning of August for a vacation. I hadn't wanted to go. My grandmother, a pinched-up bird-like woman with sunken eyes and a thin hard mouth, made me nervous. Her face always looked as if it were in the shadows. She wore silk housedresses, a hair net, and too much powder and rouge.

Her favorite name for me was "Mr. Smarty-pants." She pronounced "smarty" as "smeerty." If I accidentally spilled something on her velvet sofa, or tracked mud onto her oak floors, or dropped a glass as I was carrying it to the kitchen, she always said, in a faintly disgusted voice, as if she'd known all along that it would happen, "Well, Mr. Smeerty-pants. Look what you've done now."

Her house was huge and angular, with a spiral staircase to the second floor, a basement that smelled of must and decay, and an attic full of cobwebs and dry rot. I had never been in the back bedroom before. It seemed somehow set off from the rest of the house, a place from which, if you went there, you might not come back.

My grandmother never left the house. She didn't have to. Elm Grove was a small town, and people looked in on her periodically. The local market delivered groceries weekly, and the Presbyterian minister called often. The walls were filled with faded pictures of Jesus with his boyish face, wispy beard, and long brown hair, and with needlework homilies and commandments: *Honor thy father and thy mother, Remember the Sabbath day to keep it holy, God bless this house.*

I hadn't wanted to come. I would have preferred to stay in St. Louis with my friends and play baseball in the streets of the bright new suburb where we'd lived for the past five years. The white sidewalks, the neat familiar brick ranch houses, the meticulous lawns and small trees

talking

seemed so much friendlier than these towering frame structures, the looming oaks, the old folks sitting on benches in the town square.

We were only supposed to stay two weeks, but my father had had a severe reaction to a new sulfa drug he was taking. I wasn't sure how severe. He had had multiple sclerosis for about five years and we had come to expect sudden alterations in his health.

Years ago he had wanted to be a baseball player, and had been playing semipro ball when the dizzy spells began. He would be out in center field waiting for a long fly when suddenly the ball would begin to dance back and forth crazily, multiplying itself in midair, until he couldn't tell which ball was the ball. He'd have to guess, and, more often than not, he'd guess wrong. At first it was comical, my mother said, the team ribbing him about his uncharacteristic clumsiness. But soon he was off the team, and people in town were talking behind his back about alcoholism as he weaved down the sidewalk on his unsteady legs.

When the disease was finally diagnosed, we moved to St. Louis because the doctors thought that a warm climate might bring about a remission. For five years he tried every experimental treatment they gave him, but the disease gradually deepened, and he had recently progressed from a cane to crutches. He had been on the experimental sulfa drug for several days with no appreciable side effects. We were sitting at dinner, my grandmother chewing her small food carefully and noiselessly, my mother distracted, my father hunched over his plate.

Suddenly, my father's arm swept across the table, knocking me backward in my chair. "Elbows *off* the table!" he snapped.

I hadn't realized that my elbows were on the table; it was one of the little things I did that drove him crazy. Lately, most of the things I did seemed to drive him crazy.

"Jim," my mother said.

"Go ahead," my father said. "Take his side again. You always do."

My mother looked hurt.

My grandmother stared at her plate, chewing. "Mr. Smeerty-pants," she said to her spinach.

My father grabbed his crutches, which were propped on the wall beside him, and pulled himself up from the table. "Well, pardon me for living," he said, and stalked off.

"It's okay, Petey," my mother said. "Your father's not feeling very well today."

When the crash resounded from the next room, my mother was up from the table and in the living room and I was behind her before I had time to think. My father was sprawled on the floor, one crutch flung in a corner with a broken lamp, one poking awkwardly from beneath him like a bone.

"Jesus," my mother said.

"Just leave me alone," he said.

That night boils broke out all over his body, his temperature rose to 104 degrees, and he began urinating blood. The town physician was chagrined.

"You didn't tell me he was allergic to sulfa drugs," he said.

"We didn't know," my mother said.

"Well, now we do," he said.

Shortly after my father moved to the back bedroom he called me in with a "business proposition." He said he

talking

would pay me a dollar a day to empty the large jug of urine at his bedside. He was so weak that he couldn't get out of bed to use the bathroom, and he didn't want my mother to have to do it.

"What do you say?" he said.

I was twelve, it was 1956, a dollar seemed like a lot of money, and I didn't think I really had a choice in the matter. It seemed less a request than a duty.

"Okay," I said.

I emptied the jug twice a day—once in the morning and once in the evening. It was heavy, and the sluggish mixture of blood and pus and urine made me queasy. The jug was attached to a catheter tube that disappeared up under the sheets. I'd pull the tube out of the jug and put it in a silver urinal, the tube still dripping fluid. The jug itself was heavy, like a cider jug, and although I'd try to hold it away from my body as I carried it to and from the bathroom, I usually ended up hugging it to me to keep it from slipping. It was sticky, and my clothes retained the faint sickly smell.

"Is there anything you want to talk about?" my father would say.

September came with its clarity and dust, the cornstalks outside of town turning yellow and brittle in the dry wind. The frogs at old man Miller's pond grew quiet, and the cricket song subsided in the long nights.

My father was improving slowly, but he couldn't be moved. My mother suggested that rather than miss the first weeks of school, I might attend the local grade school with a neighbor boy I'd gotten to know. We'd mowed lawns together during August, which had been wet and lush, each taking one side of the heavy rusted push mower's handle, and, with all of our strength, forcing the blades through the thick grass. We got paid a quarter apiece for each job, and we immediately spent it on root beer floats at the soda fountain of Williamson's Drugs on the square. The root beer floats were fifteen cents, but Mr. Williamson always gave us two for a quarter, and we usually drank both at one sitting.

Old Mr. Williamson had copies of *Playboy* magazine behind the counter, and he liked to pull them out when nobody was in the store and flash them by us.

"Give you boys an education," he said. "I could tell you things about your mom and pop, too."

"Like what?" I said.

"I remember Violet," he said. "She worked for me, you know. Scooped ice cream behind the soda fountain. She came in here a puny girl, and I made a woman of her. You should have seen the muscles she got scooping ice cream.

"I remember your pop, too. He used to come in here all the time with his buddies. Goofing around, mostly. Never bought anything but ice cream. I wondered why he was in here so often, and only when Violet was working.

"Then one day I was in back stocking shelves and I saw him come in and order ice cream. I was behind him, so I could see your mother from his perspective. When she bent down to scoop the ice cream, her blouse hung down and you could look right in. You know, that's what your father was doing, getting her to bend over so he could look down her blouse." He laughed. "Bet you didn't know that about your pop."

Anything you want to talk about? my father said.

No, I said.

talking

"One time," Mr. Williamson continued, "he ran off to Chicago. Your mother's brother, Wilford, had to drive down there and get him. Found him in some whorehouse drunk or something. Wonder why she married him. A nice girl, Violet. Her father the church organist and all. He didn't like it much, but what can you do? These kids."

When I told my mother about it, she shook her head. "Don't listen to him," she said. "Mr. Williamson's lonely. And he just likes to make up stories."

I started school with Norman. It was on the other side of town, across the square, a farm implement store on one side and cornfields on the other. I was smaller than most of the kids there, but smarter. They were doing work I'd done the year before. They talked slow, had no sideburns, had never heard of Elvis, and thought Eisenhower was great. They all wore little buttons printed in red, white, and blue: "I Like Ike." While they giggled and talked together, I sat by myself, watching.

Outside at recess I watched them play football. I'd never played football in St. Louis, and I wasn't sure I could. When Norman finally dragged me into the game, he told me I was the blocker. And for several days at recess I stood on the line, confused and self-conscious, getting knocked down and trampled on every play.

One afternoon, when we stopped at Williamson's on the way home from school, something seemed different. We were the only ones in the drugstore. Mr. Williamson was mopping the counter with a damp rag. The air seemed charged.

"The root beer boys," he said. And then to me, "You know, kid, your grandma ain't your real grandma. Anyone tell you that? I suppose not."

I took the ball and ran for a touchdown. And for the rest of the week, every time they handed me the ball, I'd run up the middle, knocking down tacklers all the way to the goal line. "He's pretty good," they said.

The Friday before we were to leave for St. Louis, I stopped at Williamson's Drugs. My mother had told me not to, but I wanted to see Mr. Williamson again, to find out what he meant.

"Forget it, kid," he said. "I shouldn't have said anything."

"But I want to know."

"Have a root beer on me," he said.

At dinner that night my father was cheerful. "Well, Petey boy, I guess you'll be glad to get to St. Louis and your friends. Hasn't been much of a summer for you, I'm afraid. How was school today?"

"Okay," I said.

"What kind of answer is that?" he said.

"A short one," I said.

My mother laughed.

"Mr. Smeerty-pants," my grandmother said.

Years later, after my father died, I did find out what Mr. Williamson meant. My grandmother had been moved to a nursing home, her feet fat boats of cancer. My mother and I were cleaning out her house, and I found a packet of letters in the attic—correspondence between my grandfather, Robert, who had died of a stroke when my father was twelve, and his brother, Vergil, a farmer in Minnesota. In the dusty gloom of the quiet attic I pieced the story together.

Vergil had been married to Anna for ten years and had

talking

three children when Maureen came to work for him as a farmhand. Maureen was young and attractive, and Anna was increasingly moody and depressive. Vergil began sleeping with Maureen. When he confessed that he had gotten Maureen pregnant, Anna hanged herself from a rafter in the barn.

Maureen went to Minneapolis to have the baby, and Vergil, feeling that it would be unwise for him to marry Maureen and acknowledge the child and the cause of Anna's death, asked his brother, Robert, for help. Robert, a lawyer in Elm Grove, offered to adopt the child since his own wife, Virginia, had been unable to bear him any children. Virginia, who had gained the reputation in town of being "peculiar," soon began telling everyone that the child was really hers. In time, she came to believe it.

On his deathbed, Robert told my father the truth: that "Aunt" Maureen was really his mother, and that "Uncle" Vergil was really his father, and that Virginia was no relation to him at all. After Robert's death Virginia insisted that the story was untrue and she was his real mother. Rumors spread around town, and whenever other kids wanted to enrage my father, they'd call him a bastard.

My mother corroborated the story as we packed the pictures of Jesus and the needlework homilies into boxes for the auctioneer.

"It was hard for him," she said. "By the time we were seniors in high school, he knew that the story was true. Our families were very religious, and Jim thought I'd never marry him if I knew. He thought somehow the whole thing was his fault. I said it didn't matter. But all his life it ate at him. He thought the multiple sclerosis was God's punishment for his sin. He worried about you. I wish he could have talked to someone about it. Once he got sick we never really talked much about anything. I don't think he talked much with anyone about anything."

Is there something you want to talk about? my father was always asking me, propped up in bed, slumped over in his wheelchair, sitting at the kitchen table, glancing up over his glasses and his newspaper.

The question irritated me, made me taciturn and sullen. It irritated me and seemed like such an effort. I had to be out in the streets playing ball with the guys, or upstairs doing homework, or off somewhere with my girlfriend, or going to graduate school, or making money. It irritated me, and anyway, I had nothing I wanted to say to him, and there was never enough time for talking.

Now I'm talking, talking. And there's all the time in the world.

the little woman

"One of these days," Alfie Prince was saying, "I'll have to take you home to meet the little woman."

I was standing across the long table from him, on the third floor of the Carlee Dress Factory in St. Louis, Missouri. The room was huge and poorly lit, fluorescent shop lamps hanging over the wooden tables where each two-man team worked. I had gotten the job for the summer because my father's friend, Mr. Goldberg, was vice president of the company. We didn't need the money, but my father thought I should contribute toward college in the fall.

It was 1962, and the factory, which produced expensive women's clothes and advertised in *Vogue* and *Harper's Bazaar*, had not yet modernized its facilities. Rather than fire the workers who had been there for decades, the company executives had opted to delay installation of automated equipment, and allow the old workers to ease out gracefully. As the older workers retired, they were replaced with temporary high school and college students. Eventually the whole place would be automated.

Alfie Prince rolled his false teeth around in his mouth. "Yeah," he said. "You'd like the little woman." He had pulled his baggy trousers down around his knees and was adjusting his soiled jockstrap. The first time I had seen him do that I had been startled, but hadn't said anything. Having watched him perform the same operation daily for six weeks now, I still couldn't tell if the stained appliance needed adjusting or if he was just showing off for the women who sat in one dim corner, tying thin pieces of cloth together that were too short to use but too long to throw away. The older women stared placidly at their work, while two of the younger ones giggled.

Alfie threw a glance across his hunched shoulder. "You like the women?" he asked me.

Our job, day after day, was to heft the heavy bolts of material from under the long tables where they were stored, remove the brown wrapping, roll them the length of the table—one man on each side—and then cut the fabric to size. Each of the younger guys was assigned to work with one of the older and more experienced men. I worked with Alfie Prince, and Mr. Goldberg's son, Bobby, worked with Harry Crawford.

Alfie was dark and balding, with a huge nose and a beat-up pockmarked face. He seemed always to be adjusting something—his false teeth, his jock strap, his gray T-shirt that drooped down to his chest. When he talked, it was as if he were talking to some invisible presence just off to the right of you or somewhere in the middle distance. Perhaps he was nervous, I thought, or perhaps he just needed glasses.

Harry was short, with a graying burr haircut and horn-rimmed glasses. He wore bermuda shorts that went to his knees, and striped madras shirts that clashed. He was color blind, but fascinated with the names of the colors for this year's fashions. "Cranberry," he'd say, "cranberry," as if it were a wonderful observation, something strange and amazing. And "mahogany," "chartreuse," "cerulean."

Bobby had warned me that these men, who had spent so many years in the factory, were threatened by the young replacements. They didn't like the idea that some young kid could come in and do their job as well as, or better than, they could after just a couple of days.

"Never cut all the way across the table with your scissors," Bobby warned. "Let *them* cut two-thirds of the way across, and *you* cut one-third. And never try to carry a bolt of material by yourself. Let them carry it, or, if you do carry it, always ask for help, and drag your end down near the floor as if it's too heavy. You got to work with them all summer. You might as well get along."

After six weeks of it, however, I was ready to do almost anything to relieve the slow boredom.

"What the hell are you doing?" said Alfie Prince. "Look, you dumb fuck, what you made me do."

The material was stretched out before us, the long metal bar marking our cutting line. I had been cutting faster than Alfie, and, trying to beat me to the middle, he had cut a gash sideways across the bar.

"Now the goddamn piece is ruined." He glared at me, rolling his teeth. "Watch the hell what you're doing," he said.

I nodded, and from then on there was a silent competition between us to see who could cut to the middle with his flashing scissors first. I easily won whenever I wanted to, cutting swiftly and surely almost through to his side before he'd even begun. But to make it interesting I'd usually give him a handicap, letting him get almost to the middle before I'd start and then speeding along to the finish line. It drove him crazy. "Sorry," I'd tell him. "I forgot." Or, "I'm going as slow as I can." And then I'd race him to the next bolt of material and heft it easily into place myself. "It's okay, Alfie," I'd say. "I don't need any help."

My father was amused when I recounted the day's competition to him at dinner. "But take it easy with the old man," he said. "He's not been as privileged as you."

One day toward the end of the summer, the ceiling fans stirring the heavy St. Louis humidity and heat into dark pools of sluggishness, Mr. Goldberg called Bobby and me into his office. Shit, I thought. Alfie had finally complained. Mr. Goldberg's office was bright and comfortable, a small velvet couch and two upholstered chairs on one side and his large oak desk on another. The grayish-blue carpeting was plush and new. Mr. Goldberg motioned to the couch.

"Sit down, men," he said. "I need some help from you. I need an expert opinion." He nodded to a door at the back of his office where two young models had just entered. They were probably six or seven years older than we were, maybe twenty-four or twenty-five. "Ladies," he said, "could you try on these dresses for us?" He motioned to a rack by the wall. On it were perhaps a dozen dresses, in the fabrics I'd been handling all summer. "Thought you boys might like to see the end product of your work. And you can tell me what you think of these new styles. You can be my product marketing advisors."

The models were slipping out of their own dresses and lifting the samples from the rack. I looked at Bobby, who just smiled. Dressed only in flimsy slips and bras, the models wriggled expertly into the sample dresses as I gaped.

"Well, men. And what do you think?" Mr. Goldberg said.

I swallowed and nodded. Bobby said he thought they were nice. He liked them fine.

"Okay, ladies," Mr. Goldberg said. "Now these styles are made to cling tight, so no undergarments." He looked at us and winked. "It's the latest thing, the wave of the future. They're burning their bras out there."

The models stepped out of the dresses and slips, unhooking their bras and draping them over the rack. They were business-like and efficient, as if they did this sort of thing every day.

I felt myself flushing, my breath coming fast, my heart beating loud enough for anyone to hear. I glanced at Bobby. He seemed relaxed and amused.

"Well, men. And what do you think?" Mr. Goldberg said.

We said we thought they were fine.

Later, as Alfie and I were rolling the bolts out on the table, the fabric had a new feel to me, somehow softer, silkier. I worked in slow motion.

"That's better," Alfie Prince said. "You're doing better today, kid. No need to bust your ass over this stuff. What did the boss want, anyway?"

When I told him, offhandedly but in glowing detail, Alfie stopped work, pursed his lips, and leaned forward on the table, rolling his teeth. "Well, I'll be goddamned. You little suck," he said. Then he dropped his pants and adjusted his jock. "You come over tonight, kid, and I'll introduce you to the little woman."

Over at the next table Harry was marveling. "Magenta. Tangerine. Flamingo."

At five o'clock we punched out and Alfie offered me a ride home. I didn't really want to go with him, but one of those intense afternoon thunderstorms that St. Louis is so famous for had just burst over the city, and I didn't want to wait in the rain for the bus.

Alfie's car was a beat-up '54 Chevy, the ashtray crammed with butts, the windshield yellow and hazy. We drove through the gray city rain in silence, Alfie leaning against his door, his arm propped on the window.

"So you like women?" he said finally, rolling his teeth and leering. "You ever had a woman?" he asked. "You know what's good? You get a real hot day in August, you crank up the old fan and set a pan of ice right in front of it and aim it at the bed. Then you get in with your woman and sweat. And the sweat blows cool and breezy. It's great, kid. Look, you stop by the house for a drink, meet the little woman."

Alfie Prince's house was a small one-story white frame box in the run-down southern part of the old suburb where we lived, about two miles from our own large house. The neighborhood seemed somehow tired and stingy, as if the houses sagged on their small lawns, clutching the broken sidewalks to them.

"Home, sweet home," Alfie said.

The front door opened straight into the living room, with its gold shag carpet, its hide-a-bed and La-Z-Boy

the little woman   19

recliner, its console TV.

"What can I get you?" he said. "You drink whiskey?"

"Sure," I lied.

We drank whiskey as the storm raged outside, a thick rain pelleting the windowpanes.

"So you think you're pretty hot stuff," Alfie said after a couple of whiskeys and some small talk about the factory. "The boss's pal, eh? Mr. High Muckamuck, is that it?"

I started to get up.

"Sit down, kid. I been working in that factory longer than you been alive, and I know a thing or two. I'm pretty goddamn special, too. I got something you ain't probably never seen. I got the little woman."

"Where is your wife, Alfie?" I said, looking nervously around the room. If I had taken the bus I would have been home, having dinner in our quiet kitchen.

He laughed. "Drink up, kid," he said. "Free whiskey."

"I think I've got to get home," I said.

"Relax, kid. It's raining. I want you to meet the little woman. I'll drive you home in a minute. Yeah, the little woman. She's stuck by me all these years, through thick and through thin. That's what we all need, kid, someone to stick by us. You know, things might be going bad at work, or you might feel that some other guy was getting special treatment, you might feel dumb or stupid, but you got someone to stick by you, kid, and everything's okay."

I nodded. "Alfie ..."

"Someone to stick by you, kid. Harry, he ain't got nobody. I got the little woman. Come on and meet her." He reached over roughly and grabbed my arm. The whiskey had made me unsteady and I wavered a bit.

"What's the matter, kid? You don't look so good. Come on in here and meet her." He had opened the door to the bedroom and was pushing me in. The door closed with a click behind me.

It was dark in the room with all the shades drawn. I could hear the rain slamming down hard on the tin roof. I steadied myself and looked around. A large dresser, painted black, loomed in one corner, a brick stuck under one leg. A metal lamp protruded in the other corner. Magazines littered the floor—*Gent, Nugget, Swank, Dude.*

"Mrs. Prince?" I said.

And then I saw her: lying in the rusted metal bed on the far side of the room, an emaciated, nearly nude figure, dirty blonde hair draped over the pillow, one arm sagging across her gray chest, one arm hanging over the side. Perhaps she was drunk, or sleeping. I backed away from the exposed flat breasts, the eyelids aflutter with stupor or dream, the sheet creased up between the legs. Out in the living room I could hear Alfie Prince laughing.

"Hey, Mr. Hot-shot Dressmaker," he shouted through the door. "What do you think of that action? Take your time, kid. She ain't in a hurry. She's got a whole wardrobe in the closet. Mahogany, chartreuse, cerulean. You can dress and undress her. Hey, Mr. Bolt Carrier, Mr. Fast Scissors. I bet you can do a lot more."

the night nurse

We were sitting in the front row of the funeral parlor chapel, organ fugues piped in from somewhere, invisibly, like mood music in some bad film. The room was a dull gray-green, and everything seemed heavy—the deep pile carpeting, the velveteen drapes, the plush pads on all the dark mahogany pews. There was a slightly musty smell in the room, as if everyone were wearing rented clothes.

The small chapel was about half full, with people I recognized from church years ago, and a few old neighborhood friends. Most of them hadn't seen my father for years—since he'd moved to the nursing home. He was just forty-five when he moved; his multiple sclerosis had become too much for my mother to care for. I don't know why I was so angry at them. I couldn't have expected them to visit him out there, twenty miles west of the city. But I was angry anyway—at the place, the morticians, the solemn blank on everybody's face that passed for sympathy.

The minister was giving a short memorial sermon, the kind that he probably used whenever he had to speak about someone he didn't know. It included the usual platitudes, with my father's first name inserted at appropriate moments to personalize it. He was a new minister; the old one, Reverend Helmuth, had recently been committed to a Presbyterian home himself. Manic depression, marital infidelity, and a lifelong crisis of conscience and doubt had finally caused him to break down, and be forcibly retired. I remembered once, when I was in high school and he was counseling me to stay in the church, he had confessed that he himself didn't believe many of the church's teachings, that he would have liked to challenge the congregation some, but that he felt constrained to keep up appearances "for the old folks." It gave them comfort. He was good at keeping up appearances, with his massive body, his booming voice, his confident demeanor. I was glad to hear that he shared all my skepticism, but his confession merely made me more adamant about not attending church. I told my father that the minister was a fraud and that I wasn't going to church anymore. Every Sunday morning there was either anger or sadness in the house.

Now I wished that Reverend Helmuth was in the chapel pulpit, his rich voice filling the air with memory and comfort, rather than this pale, balding stranger with his thin voice that cracked more with nervousness than grief. He didn't know my father. In fact, no one there really knew my father or my mother anymore, except perhaps Eddie Hawkins, who was at my mother's side.

Eddie had been seeing my mother for several years,

mostly at the nursing home where he was on the administrative staff and my father had spent his last days. My mother said she and Eddie had so much in common, that no one else understood what it was like all those years. I didn't like him. He was a small, round man, with red cheeks and breath that smelled of pipe tobacco and sensen. I had tried to be pleasant to him for my mother's sake, but it was difficult. He always managed to say exactly the wrong thing, as he did now—how natural my father looked (he looked artificial and waxen, they had parted his hair on the wrong side and pinned a mum to his lapel—he hated mums), how sorry he was that it had happened but it was probably for the best, how everything was now in God's hands, how our faith would comfort us.

"My mother says that you've been a real help to her," I offered.

"She couldn't have done it without me," he said.

But my anger finally wasn't directed at Eddie—or the gray-green room, the practiced sincerity of the morticians, the new minister intoning from the pulpit, the faces arranged behind me with their own larger concerns—it was directed against God. Why had He let this happen? Why had He made my father suffer for all those years? Why had He let him die? And against myself. Why hadn't I been a better son? I thought of my father, slumped over in his wheelchair, sitting at the rest home, day after day, alone. Although he was a young man, the disease had virtually paralyzed him and he had to be in the chronics section of the home, with patients who were usually comatose. Most of my father's roommates died within weeks after they were admitted. What had he thought about, all those months, as he sat there listening to the raspy breathing of strangers?

There was a feeble cry somewhere behind us, a muffled thump as of something heavy being dropped, a collective gasp, and then the sounds of activity—people rising, pews creaking, programs rustling. The minister looked up, confused. I glanced at my mother, but she didn't turn around. An usher leaned up behind Eddie and whispered to us. Old Mr. Harley had collapsed, perhaps a heart attack. I was stunned. I hoped he was all right, but it was an outrage, I thought. This was my father's moment, this was our grief, and now it was interrupted, diffused. I could feel the sympathy in the room shifting to the back, as my father, my mother, and I were now somehow implicated in Mr. Harley's collapse. Several ushers carried Mr. Harley out and the service continued, but the center was gone. I could feel the eyes on me from behind, I could sense the minds wandering. Even in death my father was going to be ignored, alone, abandoned.

When the service was over, people grouped nervously, talking, I supposed, about Mr. Harley. I heard fragments of conversation. Would he be all right? It was just the heat. Where had they taken him? Almost no one stopped to talk to my mother, who stood next to Eddie, staring forward, her hand limp in his.

I glanced up toward the open casket. There, surrounded by birds of paradise and mums, standing over my father, her red cloth coat not quite covering her white uniform, was Roberta, the night nurse who had been my father's favorite. She had been at the home the day my father first arrived, and he felt that she had selected him as her special patient. She spent time with him every day, he said, and treated him better than anyone else. We had humored him, for we knew, of course, that she was just doing her job.

the night nurse

But here she was, a lone figure bending over the casket, her coat and dress lifting with her shoulders, exposing the backs of her white-stockinged legs. I had talked to her on occasion at the home, but never really paid her much attention. She was an attractive black woman, in her late thirties, perhaps, and she must have stopped at the service on her way to work. She worked nights and was, I suspected, due there now. Perhaps she had taken off, just to come see my father. She seemed to be doing something as she leaned over the casket, but I couldn't tell what. Her shoulders were moving; perhaps she was crying.

As I moved toward the casket, she turned, smiled at me, bowed her head, and was gone. I looked at my father. He seemed more peaceful now, more natural, as if he would sit up and say all those long sad years were a joke after all. And then I saw. His hair was parted on the right side now, and the little flower was gone. I turned to look toward the chapel entrance and thought I could see, through the small klatches of people, the night nurse departing, her body leaning forward as if she were pushing something hurriedly out the door, as if she had my father before her, fast in his wheelchair, rolling on his squeaky wheels toward heaven.

wordplay

I run a small vanity press. It's located on a back street on the east side of town, a working-class neighborhood of one-story, two-bedroom tract houses built in the fifties when the meatpacking plant moved its operations here. On one side of me is a furniture refinishing shop called "Wooden It Be Nice," and across the street there's a brick Presbyterian church. The furniture refinishing shop has a pine board sign with a ladder-back wooden chair suspended from it. The church has a large message board, the kind with removable letters. Each week the pastor changes the message to suit the season or his whim, I'm never sure which. Right now, for example, it's mid-December and the sign reads, "Rejoice, for Christ's Sake!" Last summer the sign read, "Wise men still seeketh Him." It's the kind of thing my father used to say, in those difficult days before he moved to the rest home. We'd be riding along in the car, going to Bob's Shopper Stopper to pick up some item—breath mints, deodorant, Vaseline—and he'd turn to me and say, "You know, sometimes I think: Woe be to he who blasphemes." I was never quite sure what I was supposed to answer, so I usually smiled, and that seemed to satisfy him. We didn't talk much.

It's surprising how much people will pay to see something they've written in print. Mr. Yi, for one, has paid me six hundred dollars over the past few months for poetry chapbooks, or "poem-books" as he calls them. Mr. Yi is a visiting scholar at the University (where I am a graduate student in history), here for a year to study the works of Thomas Pynchon and to translate his own poems into English. When he brought me his first job last summer, a chapbook of six of his poems, it was obvious he wanted more than a printing arrangement.

"Mr. Peterson Kingsley," he began in his broken English, "you are a famous publisher. I have heard of your Vi King Books, your Random Mouse Press. I have read your famous works."

I laughed. "Mr. ..."

"Yi Shin Wook."

"Mr. Wook," I began again, but he interrupted.

"No, no. Yi," he said.

"Ah. Mr. Yi. I think you've made a mistake. I'm a printer, not a publisher. The name Vi King and Random Mouse are something of a joke." I'd once thought they were inspired, a stroke of genius. They enabled my clients to imply that their books had been published by Viking, by Random House. "You see, my mother's name is Violet, and ..."

"Ha, ha," said Mr. Yi. "You are a famous publisher. You could perhaps introduce me to Mr. Thomas Pynchon.

I would very much like to meet Mr. Thomas Pynchon."

"Mr. Yi. You misunderstand. I am not a famous publisher, and no one can meet Thomas Pynchon. In fact, there are no recent photographs of Thomas Pynchon, and some people doubt his existence. And even if he does exist, I don't know him."

"Ha, ha, Mr. Peterson Kingsley. You are very funny. You will introduce me to Mr. Thomas Pynchon?"

I have now published three of Mr. Yi's "poem-books" at two hundred dollars a throw, and he keeps coming.

"You will maybe introduce me to Mr. J.D. Salinger," he says. "You will introduce me to Mr. Saul Bellow?"

He is translating Pynchon's *V* into Korean. He had wanted to translate Jacqueline Susann, but the Korean government, which is funding his visit to America, insisted on Pynchon.

"Ms. Jacqueline Susann," he says, "is perhaps not serious enough?"

He is having some difficulty, however, with Pynchon's language. The first sentence, he tells me, was particularly difficult: "Benny Profane, yo-yo, schlemiel …"

"In Korea, we have no word for yo-yo," he says. "So I see a yo-yo is something that goes away from and comes back to. I translate, 'Benny Profane, he who goes away from and comes back to.' We also have no word for schlemiel …"

I live in a small apartment above my shop. It is an efficiency, furnished very sparsely, but adequate to my needs. I am a meticulous man, and, although I go out of my way for no one and have no friends or family nearby since my father died, I am fair and honest. I tell my clients what they can expect from me, and I do everything I promise. I do much of my work by correspondence. It is neater that way. I got into this business three years ago when I started my Ph.D. in history and couldn't get a teaching assistantship. I had worked for a printing company to help pay for college, producing, among other things, books by amateur writers—family histories, autobiographies, poetry collections. Having written poetry myself and published in some little magazines, and knowing the attraction of seeing oneself in print, I thought I might set up a shop myself, specializing in that sort of thing. I took out some small ads in national writers' magazines: "Publisher looking for manuscripts. Vi King and Random Mouse imprints. Write Peterson Kingsley, Printer." The ads brought a flurry of inquiries, some from college kids who liked the puns but didn't have the money, some from elderly lady-poets handwritten on scented paper. I moonlighted weekends using the shop's equipment, and finally leased my own place. My modest trade flourished.

The imprints brought me some notoriety as well. Shortly after setting up the vanity operation I printed my own book under the Random Mouse / Vi King imprint, a book that became something of a bestseller on campuses around the country. I wrote my own blurbs praising the book outrageously, and signed famous authors' names (comically altered) to them. I printed these on the back cover, on flyers I sent to major universities, and in ads I took out in a number of prestigious literary magazines. Orders flooded in.

Because of its satiric and arguably pornographic depiction of these well-respected and influential authors, the book stimulated considerable protest, including curt letters from the legal departments of two powerful New York publishers. The phrases "defamation of character," "copyright infringement," and "cease and desist" were conspicuously repeated. One well-known novelist with a particularly masculine name threatened to close me down with his bare hands. I retired the Random Mouse / Vi King imprints. I printed retractions. I promised publicly never to appropriate an author's good name again. I can't say the whole affair exactly hurt my business, but I have been scrupulously careful since. My father was particularly distressed. "Thou shalt not lie down in green pastures," he said.

Mr. Yi is here on a grant from the Korean government. Apparently the University will agree to sponsor Koreans as visiting scholars if they can get a grant from their government and if they can demonstrate that they have enough money to support themselves in the United States. The Korean government will only give scholars grants for this purpose if they can first secure a letter of invitation from an American university.

"It is what you call a catch-22," says Mr. Yi to me one day in the shop, his new "poem book" manuscript open on the counter between us. "You will introduce me to Mr. Joseph Heller?" he asks.

What Mr. Yi did, and what many Korean visiting scholars do, was to have all of his relatives put their money in his Korean bank account. He had his bank forward a statement to the university here, demonstrating that he had enough money to support himself. The University sent him a letter of invitation, promising him a title and library privileges, and the Korean government gave him a grant. He returned the money to his relatives, and, using most of his grant money for plane tickets, flew himself and his wife and children to the United States. No one at the university seems to know that he's here, and I'm not sure how he's managing financially. Somehow I doubt that he's selling his poetry.

Today Mr. Yi surprises me with an invitation. "You will come to dinner?" he asks in a tone that is more of a statement than a question.

"I don't know, Mr. Yi," I begin, not sure I want to complicate our business relationship.

"You come at 6:00? That is good American time for dinner?"

Mr. Yi lives in a new apartment complex across town. Construction is still under way, and the grounds around the building are heaped with rubble. Billboards announcing substantial rent incentives have attracted several foreign families, but most of the units are empty. Mr. Yi is waiting for me in front of the building, shifting from foot to foot on the new sidewalk beside a tangle of wire mesh and two-by-fours.

"Ah, Mr. Peterson Kingsley," he says. "Come. Come."

The apartment already seems run-down. Tufts of lint drift in the orange shag carpeting. The plasterboard walls are smudged, and several vinyl moldings have pulled back from the baseboards. An old formica dining room table, its legs rusted, sits in the middle of the room, surrounded by a set of metal kitchen chairs. On the make-shift couch sit four children, ranging from maybe three to ten years in age. One by one they stand up and introduce themselves.

"I am Yi Joo Young," says one girl.

"I am Yi Soo Kyeong," says another.

"I am Yi Yu Jeong," says the third.

"Young Hoo!" shouts the smallest, a boy.

All three smile self-consciously and then file into the bedroom at the back, where a TV is turned on to cartoons. "He Man!" shouts the littlest over his shoulder as the door shuts behind him.

Mrs. Yi is an attractive woman, slight, though somehow more substantial than Mr. Yi. She is wearing a flower-print dress, tied at the middle, and her roundness contrasts with his angularity.

"My wife—Mrs. Yi," he smiles proudly.

Before I can reply, she is back in the kitchen, which is full of steam or smoke. The vent fan is whirring halfheartedly.

"You will drink beer?" says Mr. Yi. "We make."

I remain awkwardly in the doorway for a moment, until Mr. Yi motions for me to sit down in one of the metal chairs at the table. Mrs. Yi begins bringing out dishes. They are strange combinations of shrimp, beef, chicken, vegetables.

"You try this?" he says.

I take a small taste of the shrimp dish and smile appreciatively, waiting for Mr. Yi to help himself and Mrs. Yi to sit down. Mr. Yi gazes at me. "Eat. Eat," he says.

"You have some," I say. "And what about Mrs. Yi?"

He looks uncomfortable. "No, you eat," he says.

More steaming dishes appear on the table as the bedroom door opens. "Masters of the Universe!" shouts Young Hoo. The door shuts.

"We talk about Mr. Thomas Pynchon now?" Mr. Yi says.

And we do, in a manner of speaking, talk about

Thomas Pynchon for the next hour as I pick at the food displayed on the table before me like a page out of *The Korean Gourmet*. Mr. Yi eats nothing, and Mrs. Yi hovers somewhere between kitchen and table, invisible.

After dinner Mr. Yi suggests we take a walk. It is a beautiful spring night, clear and cool, some crocuses and daffodils improbably poking their heads through the rubble. Mr. Yi walks very close to me, bumping into me occasionally, and Mrs. Yi lags behind. I slow my pace so that Mrs. Yi can catch up—she is probably ten steps behind us now—but as I do, Mr. Yi speeds up. We are walking single file now, Mr. Yi in the lead, me following him, and Mrs. Yi following me. When we reach a street corner, Mr. Yi nudges me forward, closing his wife off behind us. As I step back to join her, he steps back simultaneously, as does she. We walk in single file around the block.

"Mr. Yi," I call to him.

He pauses for me to catch up. His wife pauses behind us.

"You ate nothing for dinner," I say. "Mrs. Yi ate nothing."

Mr. Yi looks away, distractedly, and then back to me. He eyes me curiously. "It is custom in Korea," he says somewhat uncomfortably.

"Oh," I say.

"Maybe long time ago people have not enough for guests and selves. So serve guests first. Whatever is left, serve selves. Maybe."

"I see," I say. "And Mrs. Yi walking behind us...."

"Let us talk about Mr. J.D. Salinger," says Mr. Yi.

It is August. I haven't seen Mr. Yi since April. I suppose I should have reciprocated on his dinner invitation, but my apartment is small and I prefer not to get involved.

Business is always good in the summer. Mrs. Edna Farber-Dunham of Waterloo, Iowa, has written to order a second printing of her autobiography. She has sold out the first printing of two thousand copies, to what must be the entire population of that small town. I've also got two collections of verse from members of the poetry club in Hartland, Wisconsin, and a novelette from an underwear salesman in St. Louis.

The sign on the Presbyterian church for several weeks has read, "Love Thy Neighbor as Thyself and You will Always be in Love." The letters gleam like neon. There's a new sign on the furniture refinishing place: "Chairity begins at home." Perhaps the two establishments are having a competition. My sign stays the same: "U-Publish It." In my more cynical moments I relish the pun. I wonder if the furniture refinisher or the minister has noticed.

After a hot dry summer the weather has turned unseasonably cold and rainy. Leaves prematurely litter the streets and gutters. Mr. Yi comes through the door of the shop in his usual skittish way. I feel a bit guilty. He has grown thinner and more angular as the months have passed, until he is little more than a shadow among the shadows in the shop. His English has not improved much in his year's residence. He tells me that he would like me to do an important favor for him. The Korean government has agreed to extend his grant for another year, but he needs an official progress report and letters of support.

"I would like," he says, "a letter from Mr. Thomas Pynchon. I would like a letter from Mr. J.D. Salinger and Mr. Saul Bellow."

wordplay

"Mr. Yi," I say, "I don't know these writers. I can't help you."

"I send the Korean government my Pynchon translations, my poem-books. I tell them I meet famous American authors. I need letters. You can supply. I pay good dollars." He turns and motions toward the door where his wife and children have been waiting. They stand in a line beside him.

I stare at them, my forehead wrinkled with concern.

"Mr. Peterson Kingsley," says Mr. Yi, "you are a famous publisher of Random Mouse Press, Vi King Books. You are my best friend in America. You can make such letters. There is much trouble in Korea. I do not want to take my family back now."

I gaze out the dingy shop window. Across the street the neon church sign gleams. And then I see.

"You mean," I begin slowly, "Mr. Thom Ass-Pinchin', Mr. Jaded Salinger, Mr. Sow Belly?"

"Yes, yes," he grins. "Mr. Joseph Feller, Mr. Norm Man Maler, Mr. Robert Blah-eye!"

"Mr. Phillip Rot? Mr. Ken Queasy?"

"He Man!" shouts little Young Hoo, taking my hand.

"Masters of the Universe!" I say.

the quarry

"Oh yes, and by the way," Goff said in that slow, drawn-out manner that made everything seem sleepy and uncomplicated, trivial, a mere parenthesis, "we'll be doin' a bit of roadwork up the hill, fillin' in that ditch, makin' a cut in the road. Makin' it safer, and gettin' a bit of gravel to boot." He gestured toward the oak woods that rose abruptly behind my house to the ridge. "Shouldn't affect you much. Though we'll have to take out a few of them trees. Well, I guess a guy's got to work sometime. I better be goin'." He grinned that broad confident grin that filled his weathered face with wrinkles and exposed a glint of gold tooth. He pushed his Vern's Feed & Seed cap back on his head and ran his hand through his thinning hair. "Yep," he said, looking around him like a man who owned everything in sight. "Yep." He climbed on his tractor, revved it, and puttered up the steep gravel road in front of my house.

the quarry 37

    I should have known better than to take what he said at face value. Nothing he ever said was at face value. He was a horse trader, a con man, a gyp artist. The entire township was his shell game. When I bought my place a year ago, he drove in on his tractor to introduce himself. He never got off the tractor—an antique Farm-All—just leaned over, weathered and freckled, and extended his large meaty hand. "George Goff," he said, and then sat back up and pulled the tractor forward toward the house without waiting for my name. He drove right off the end of the driveway onto the lawn and up to the front door as I followed. "Yep. I grew up in this house," he said. "Was hopin' to buy the place myself. Could use the water." He pointed up to the barn where a spring was piped into a cement trough just outside the door. The water burbled lyrically in the breeze—one of the sweet musics that had persuaded me to buy the place. "Livin' up on the ridge I got to go pretty deep for water," Goff said.

    Goff, I later learned from Ned, my neighbor down in the hollow, had been waiting for the price to go down on the property. He hadn't believed anyone would pay that much for it. It seemed cheap to me. The house and barn and forty acres cost half what a modest house on a postage stamp lot would have cost in town. Of course, there was no plumbing or central heating, but that just made the place seem more romantic to me.

    It didn't seem romantic to Christine, who took my interest in moving to the country as an excuse for her to move in with Frank. I saw it as a kind of test of our relationship—if Christine really loved me, she'd come with me. I guess she loved Frank, or his condo. I often thought about her, through the long winter nights, alone under the icy stars, or cozy by my woodstove. But it was summer; I was busy with the garden, my chickens, the restoration of the house, and didn't miss her as much as I'd thought I might. Ned, a scrap metal dealer who sculpted odd creatures out of junk in his spare time, often stopped by for a beer, and Goff seemed omnipresent. "That's a nice barn you got there," Goff had said that first day. "A guy could put a lot of hay in that barn. You gonna put any hay in that barn?" And later: "That's a nice shed you got there, Peterson. A guy could put some equipment in that shed. You gonna put any equipment in that shed?" And then: "That's a nice pasture there. A guy could put some cows in that pasture."

Now his cows were in my pasture, his equipment in my shed, his hay in my barn, and his tractor treads scarred my yard. He was my neighbor, and I was new to the country and didn't want to make enemies. But I began to see that if I didn't assert myself more he would take over the whole place.

So when he said "a little roadwork" was about to begin on top of the ridge overlooking my house and barn, I should have been more wary. But who could have guessed, who could have imagined in their wildest dreams, what cockamamie scheme Goff had in mind this time?

The next morning when I strolled up the gravel road for my usual four-mile run around the circle of town roads—a pleasant run through cornfields, hay and alfalfa, some stands of oaks and hickories, past the Catholic church and back to my property down on the lip of the secluded hollow—the bulldozers were already at work like a plague of enormous insects out of a bad Japanese horror movie, roaming the hillside, snapping the trees in their mandibles. Fifty trees had fallen already, and the dozers were each taking out three at a time and pushing them into the ditch just above the source of my spring.

"Holy shit!" I said as I stood there in my Converse running shoes, my flimsy shorts, and my T-shirt tie-dyed by Christine in one of her arts and crafts phases.

A workman, maybe thirty or thirty-five years old, stood in the ditch with a shovel, hefting dollops of dirt and debris this way and that, at random. "A big mess, isn't it?" he said, grinning and wiping the sweat from his forehead with the back of his hand, as he climbed out of the ditch. "Goff's gone crazy this time. The man is nuts. Floyd Martin," he said, extending his hand. "The road grader. I plow you out in winter." He was a good-looking, swarthy fellow with a lot of black hair slicked back with sweat, a small tattoo of an eagle on his right biceps that rippled when he flexed it almost as if it were flying.

"What the hell are you doing?" I said.

"It's not me," Floyd said, turning his palms outward at me like a crossing guard holding back kids so the traffic can pass. "I wouldn't have done this in a million years. It's Goff. He's nuts. You know, his father went nuts like this late in his life, started doing crazy things and then shot himself. Some say Goff's following in his father's footsteps."

If Goff was crazy, I thought, he was crazy like a fox. I remembered my father's theory about Richard Nixon. When Nixon was in his heyday, before he left office in disgrace, he often seemed crazy. To make the "balance of terror" work, my father argued, the President had to persuade the Russians that he was prepared to push the button, that he was willing to engage in nuclear war. With what we know about fallout, radiation sickness, nuclear winter, and environmental catastrophe, only a crazy man would be willing to engage in nuclear war. By *appearing* crazy, Nixon was merely being a master strategist, demonstrating to the Russians his capacity for lunacy. The Russians, being sane people, wouldn't mess with a crazy man who might, at the least provocation, push the button.

A dozen more trees snapped under the dozers. Floyd waved at a shirtless man up in the nearest cab, who stopped, hopped down, and joined us.

"A real nightmare, eh?" he said, grinning, the furrows on his forehead filled with dust, his belly spilled over his blue jeans. "Don't blame us. We're just doing our job." He shook his head.

"You're breaking my heart," I said.

"Township says this road ain't safe—can't see cars coming at you over the hill, so the township levels the hill. But what they really want is the gravel. They wrap their road projects in the flag of safety. You know that cut they made up at Beckett's place?"

I knew it—a vertical cut in the road thirty feet deep, sheer rock on both sides through what had been one of the loveliest hills in the county.

"Well, the gravel from that lasted two years. They're doing the same thing here. But it's really Goff. He sold the mineral rights under the road to Fendleman, the gravel contractor. Goff gets money for land that's not his, and the township levels out his ditch for free; the township gets gravel, and we got us this big ugly cut for eternity. Glad I live eight miles north." The bulldozers buzzed and chirruped in the background. "Goff said I should knock down your fence and a dozen of your trees—township owns thirty-three feet from the center of the road—but I won't do it. No need to—don't know why he wanted it."

I wondered: Did Goff want me off the property? Was he still miffed at not getting the land? Or was he just being a good citizen—serving the town board (he was one of three members) by providing his land for their project, making the road "safe" for the half dozen vehicles that used it daily. Or did he just revel in putting his fat thumbprint on everything in sight?

"You do know," I said, "that I've got a spring just below all this carnage, not fifty yards away."

"Shit, you do?" the tattooed man said, the eagle pausing in mid-flight. "Goff didn't say nothing about that. I'd worry about that if I was you. No telling what the blasting will do. They're taking this hill down forty feet. I'd yell at Goff, if I was you. I'd call Elmer Ernst, the town board chairman."

I walked on up to Goff's place, the buzz of the bulldozers and the crack of falling trees slapping at the back of my neck. Goff already had my barn and my shed and my pasture. Now he was taking my water and my view. His towering, white house with its bright red roof and sky-blue trim loomed like an insult. I turned into his driveway where a huge white billy goat was tethered in the side yard, the ten-foot chain just long enough to allow it to reach a small empty bowl and a bucket of water. There were no trees or shade. A bevy of lawn ornaments—three dwarves, a ceramic toad, a Negro jockey with a ring in his hand, some mushrooms, and a Bambi—flanked the back porch. A smiley face was painted in red, white, and blue on the end of the huge propane gas tank.

No one was home except for a squat dog (one in a succession—dogs didn't last long at Goff's; he'd run the previous one, a gift to his wife, over with his cattle trailer) that was circling nervously, snapping and growling and shaking his shaggy head, puffing his barrel chest like a TV wrestler. I skipped the run and went back down the hill to call Elmer Ernst and then Ned.

It's amazing how everything is so underplayed, so low key, in the country. During last year's drought I'd hung out at Vern's Feed & Seed occasionally, listening to farmers: "Yep, lost my well last week, cost me four thousand dollars for a new one"; "Yep, lost eighteen head of cattle last month"; "Yep, looks like the corn didn't pollinate, crop's down seventy percent." All in an offhand, anecdotal tone as if they were talking about a sporting event.

Elmer Ernst had patiently explained the plan. They were perforating the bedrock with twenty-foot-deep holes. When the dynamite went off, cracks would form between the perforations "like a sheet of postage stamps," and then the air hammers could break up the smaller stamps of limestone into moveable chunks for the crusher. The postal metaphor, mixed as it was, put the whole mad project in a familiar, almost domestic frame. Ernst was pleasant, if grave. "We can kill two birds with one stone. We got to make that road safe for our citizens," he said. "And we need gravel." Eventually a barn-sized pile of gravel would be deposited beside the road at the top of the hill where it would supply the township's needs for two or three years. Of course, gravel trucks would be moving in and out during that period. And, no, he didn't know about my spring, and, yes, the blasting could change the flow or crack the well casing—he'd known it to happen before—but "they got insurance for that kind of thing." As if that made everything all right. "You lost both arms and legs?" I wanted to say to him. "No problem, they got insurance for that kind of thing."

Ned was equally matter-of-fact. "They never pay," he said. "They always win in court. They'll haul a seismograph down to your place before they blast, and record the readings. Legally, if the reading don't exceed a certain level, they haven't done any damage. Any damage you can show them—a cracked foundation, a dry spring, a broken window—they'll say happened before they blasted. They'll say you're just trying to get them to repair your old buildings or dig you a new well. They'll say it was the drought that stopped the spring. They'll pull out the seismograph readings in court and you won't have a leg to stand on. New construction, solid foundations, and there's usually no problem. But these old buildings, or springs, that's something else altogether. Forget it, Peterson, you're *screwed*," Ned chortled.

The next morning at 5 a.m. they started drilling holes for the dynamite. The drone of the compressor and the ratchet of the drill ground on all day like a dentist's as I went about my chores feeding my chickens, putting up a new bluebird house, replanting the strawberry bed, weeding the peas and broccoli, and trying to write.

I'd bought my place with the money I'd made selling my small press operation. Now I taught history at the college during the school year and did freelance editorial work for a textbook publisher in New Jersey in the summers. I liked the editorial job. They sent me manuscripts of middle school and high school textbooks—all subjects—and I scrutinized them for readability and wrote study questions, sometimes for inclusion in the book itself and sometimes for separate study guides. It was the kind of work I could do at home, it gave me time to read and write, and I enjoyed it.

Currently I was writing the word problems for a new eighth grade math text, but with the endless drone of the drill it was impossible to concentrate. I found myself thinking, "If a truck can remove five yards of gravel from a roadside every six minutes, how long will it take before a man running as fast as he can (figure seven miles per hour) can put it all back?" "If a seismograph reads six inches per second at the point of the blast, and the reading decreases by four-tenths inches per second for every hundred feet the shock waves travel, how much will a thirty-one-year-old man, sitting in a house one-eighth mile away, age?"

I took out the adjustable screens. I closed all the windows. I sat sweltering in the mid-summer humidity, and still the drill grated like a headache, a razor cut, hemorrhoids, a bad tooth.

The drilling went on for one week, for two. One afternoon, toward the end of the second week, I walked up to see Goff. I had not yet vented my anger about the project, about my not being consulted, about the madness of the whole enterprise, about how I couldn't think or work. When I turned into his drive, he was in his truck with a hefty slack-jawed man I took to be Fendleman. As I approached, Goff started the truck up and rolled past me with a nod, not bothering to stop. I turned, and, hands on hips, watched him rumble out of sight down the town road trailing dust and exhaust. I paused for a moment, surveying the farmstead with its shabby picket fence, its dilapidated outbuildings with their splintered red doors, its litter of lawn ornaments, its hay and weed fields stretching off the ridge into the distance, and could think only of the heap of rock and rubble, the piles of downed trees that graced the hill above my house.

I was about to leave when I heard a tapping—a woodpecker, perhaps, or something flapping in the breeze. But no, it was coming from the house. There, at the window, was Stefanie, Goff's wife—tapping at the pane. She pointed to the door and beckoned silently, mouthing "come in." I glanced down the road where the dust from Goff's truck was mixing with the dust of the drilling, and then walked to the house.

The door opened directly onto the living room with its blue indoor-outdoor carpeting, its imitation oak paneled walls, its green La-Z-Boy recliner, its 21-inch console TV, its plastic-covered side chairs, its oversized colonial couch. She was sitting on the couch in her housecoat—a floral affair with lace collar and sleeves. She was a good ten or twelve years younger than Goff—no more than forty, if that, and she was still a good-looking woman in the slightly slutty way that characterized certain rural girls. She was blonde with an abundance of black eye makeup and a small upturned nose. She was thin, beginning, perhaps, to be what one might call "bony," but not at all unattractive. How had she gotten stuck out here, isolated on the farm with the likes of Goff? She had a bruise on her left cheek, or perhaps her makeup had just smudged. Perhaps she had been crying.

"I can't take it anymore," she said in an even voice,

setting her jaw and gazing out the window. Then, looking back at me with a level gaze, she said, "Sit down," and patted the couch beside her with one hand, while unfastening the belt of her housecoat with the other.

I glanced off out the window and then back at Stefanie. Her housecoat opened on a lacy black bra and black silk culotte panties similar to some I had given to Christine one Christmas. Her legs lolled open on the couch. I swallowed. "Mrs. Goff," I began.

"Sit down," she said again, her voice flat but musical, burbling slightly like my spring.

I sat down, short of breath and queasy, desire rising ridiculously up my spine. I felt like a grade school kid sitting at his desk with a hard-on as the bell rang for recess.

I had talked to Stefanie on a number of occasions over the year that I'd owned my place—she'd brought me rhubarb and sweet corn—I'd reciprocated with strawberries and asparagus. She'd admired my bluebird houses and I'd built her one. I'd bought raffle tickets from her for the Catholic bazaar and pig roast in Lockhart. She'd told me about the previous owner of the property—Goff's aunt, who had died in the house at age ninety—and said I should stop by if I ever needed anything. Occasionally I'd seen her on the back of the tractor as Goff drove past my house on his way to my meadow where he pastured his heifers, or perched atop the hay wagon on the way to my barn with Goff's second cutting. But nothing more than that.

"He doesn't listen to anybody," she said. "He doesn't listen to me at all. Well," she said, lying back on the couch with a bored, defeated look, "what are you waiting for?"

I looked out the window toward the growing cut in

the quarry

the hillside, the falling trees; I thought about Christine back in Milwaukee with Frank, thought about Goff driving off with Fendleman, grinning, flashing his gold tooth. And somehow my jeans were at my knees and I was sinking into the couch and thinking there was more than one way to move the earth.

A week later Fendleman came, dragging his seismograph, and set off the first charge. It was a tremendous explosion, rattling the windows in the house, sending the cat flying across the room and into the wall, tossing several boulders the size of Volkswagens down the hillside. Though the old crack in the barn foundation might have widened some, and though the hay shed seemed to sag a bit more than it did before, I couldn't really discern any damage. The seismograph corroborated that. Fendleman tipped his cap, smiled pleasantly at me, and was off.

The air hammer and the rock crusher continued for several weeks; there were four smaller blasts, and then Fendleman and his crew were gone. Once again the only sounds were the wrens and bluebirds warbling in the trees, a band of sparrows nattering in the barn, the clucking of chickens in the side yard, the breeze through the remaining oaks, the apples in the old orchard ripening. I was writing questions for a psychology textbook: "Describe the famous experiment using slobbering dogs." "According to Freud, women envy what part of the male anatomy, and why?"

The pile of gravel at the top of the hill was not the size of a barn, not even the size of a small house—the original estimate, it turned out, had been too optimistic. The supply would probably last only six months, if that.

Meanwhile, the road, a narrow tunnel cut into the hillside with a hairpin turn at its center, was appreciably less safe. Somehow, I felt better about things. The gravel pile was going fast; the vegetation was growing back. And Goff was looking somehow smaller—his shoulders seemed to slump more as, from my window, I watched him hauling hay to the barn or feed to his cows.

Did Goff know about me and Stefanie? I wondered. He never showed the slightest suspicion, and she behaved no differently than she ever had before—cordial, pleasant, distant—in no way conspiratorial. I'd looked for a hint from her, a sidelong glance, perhaps, as, on my four-mile run, I passed her mowing her front yard or saw her hauling fence posts down to the pasture for Goff. But there was nothing. When I saw her, my heart always beat a little faster and my breath came shorter, my face a blush, but from her—nothing. Not that I wanted anything. Her indifference was, in fact, a relief. I'd had my small revenge on Goff, and I guess she had, too. And that was that.

One day in late September, one of those blue dry days that Wisconsin is famous for, the underbrush in the woods cleaned out, the lush grass of summer dried and neat, a hint of winter chill in the air, Goff came rumbling down the road on his tractor, the old engine backfiring and popping. He had his bib overalls on and a grimy T-shirt underneath. I had avoided him whenever possible since the incident, to the point, even, of retreating out back into my woods whenever I heard him coming, which seemed more often than ever. All I could see in his face was the deep cut in the road, the shabby scraps of gravel on the roadside, and Stefanie, skinny in her black bra and culottes. But today I breathed deep and went out to meet him. He was sitting in my driveway on his tractor, looking off down the road, preoccupied, when I approached him. When he saw me, he grinned and tipped his cap back on his head, his gold tooth glinting.

"Oh, Peterson," he drawled. "Nice to see you."

I nodded at Goff. "I've been pretty busy, I guess."

We chatted about the weather, about his hay crop, about his old tractor. We surveyed the land around us like men with all the time in the world. And then Goff came to the point.

"I been meaning to stop and see you," he said. "Let you know about my plans. Township needs more gravel. Now this other hill of mine, opposite your house? It's just going to waste—too steep for cows and them oaks is about ready to be harvested. Thought I'd clear-cut the hillside and then sell it to Fendleman. Enough gravel there to last a decade, I bet. You ever want to sell your place, I'd be interested. Well, I better be goin'. A guy's got to work."

He revved up his tractor and puttered down the hill, inflated, bigger than life again, a huge thumb poised on the horizon. I stood watching him, and then the space he left, for a full five minutes. I stood watching as the birds and the trees and the hillside went about their own small business, hard on the crumbling edge of the future.

men at work

Ned, the neighbor in the hollow, is adding a basement and a bathroom to his house. For forty years he's made do with a privy. "First thing," he roars, "city folks want to do when they move to the country is to shit indoors and eat outdoors." His wife is tough as nails and smells like sweet horse feed. He's asked me and Floyd to help "push cement." He knows there's no love lost between us; we hardly speak.

Floyd drives the big yellow road grader all summer, and in winter chainsaws trees. He's lived here all his life; he's thirty-three. I think his brain is his smallest muscle.

I come out from town every summer to write. He thinks I just sit on my duff all day and dote. He knows I couldn't knock off a three-point buck if it came straight at me, or skid a downed tree. We've fought over fence lines and hunting rights, as fiercely as any slicker and hayseed.

Now, standing in this dim room scooped out of the earth beneath Ned's house, we wrestle the handmade cedar cement chute into place as the fat driver slams back the shaft and the cement sluices down in slow motion. We slog the mix into our barrows, and shoulder it into the footings. We're working, despite ourselves, like a team, the cool gritty smell of cement adrift in this damp cup of earth.

Ned's wife, Moll, all field corn, oats, and molasses, brings us sweet spring water to drink, some hard bread and hunks of goat cheese. There is no place I'd rather be: three men in deep, making a place that will stay.

"Enough lollygaggin' around," Ned roars.

I glance over at Floyd who shoots a glance back. We lift our shovels and beat the shit out of each other. We get back to work.

cross country

Fendelman was flexing his muscles in the corner by the pool table while I downed a Pepsi at the bar. And his muscles weren't inconsiderable, I reflected in that backhand way that Melville had of emphasizing things by double negatives. Several locals hovered around him, admiringly, small spasms of laughter occasionally caroming off the walls like well-placed billiard shots. He probably hefted weights all day at his gravel operation, and I knew he did cement work on the side. He was thirty, maybe, younger than I, and confident, boasting that it was over before it started.

Actually, it was. I knew I was no match for him with my sedentary thinness bred by years of sitting at a desk reading history, or, more recently, lazing in my overstuffed chair editing textbooks. My new Vern's Feed & Seed T-shirt hung loose on my small frame, and my legs, pale and skinny, wavered in my shorts. It was, of course, a ridiculous mismatch. I thought about the wisdom of a colleague's sixtieth birthday mug: *Old age and treachery will overcome youth and skill.* Would that it were true. Maybe I could get him with the old "hey kid, yer shoelace's untied" ploy.

But, no, Fendelman wasn't as stupid as he looked. It was hard, in fact, to tell if he was stupid at all. He had that way about him some men had, of powerfully not saying things, that made him seem formidable and canny. A kind of Hemingway ethic had survived out here in the country among the farmers and blue-collar workers, where silence was itself a kind of intelligence.

But now he was talking and laughing in the corner, a pitcher of Pabst in his hand, as happy and gregarious as a pastor.

"You guys about ready?" Goff said. I set down my Pepsi, and Fendelman lifted the half-full pitcher to his mouth and drank it down.

"Yeah," he said, a tight smile on his sudsy lips, his hard face stolid, a stone.

How had I gotten involved in this foolishness, anyway? It was clear I was just the butt of a joke, a few hours' dumb entertainment. Why hadn't I thought it through? When Goff announced he would sell off to the gravel company his forty-acre parcel on the ridge opposite our house, the gravel from the roadbed project having run out, I'd made him a counteroffer. It was, of course, ridiculously low, but it was the best I could do. Goff, in his slow, deliberate way, said he'd "think on it." On the one hand he wanted the money that the gravel company could pay him; on the other, I figured he no more wanted a quarry operation in the neighborhood, not a stone's throw from his house, than I did. If Goff was anything, he was practical and self-serving; he would weigh the profit against the cost, his bank account against the quiet. For several weeks I heard nothing.

Then one day I saw Goff and Fendelman crashing through the underbrush opposite our house, checking out the property line, gesturing and shaking their heads. I thought now was as good a time as any to try to reason with him again.

When I reached the top of the ridge, Fendelman had retreated into the woods with his tape measure, and Goff was smiling pleasantly. Or was it a smirk?

"We're measuring up the property line," Goff said. "Though, of course, we'll have to do a proper survey. You'll pay half of the surveyor's fee?" he asked in what was more a statement than a question.

"You've decided then," I said.

"Your offer is pretty low," he said.

"It's the best I can do," I said.

Goff said nothing, just pursed his lips and looked off toward Fendelman in the trees. Then, "It's the best you can do?" he said.

Fendelman was tying a red flag to a dead elm. He was a big man, "the armwrestling champ of Ithaca County," Ned had said.

I paused a moment. "I guess we could armwrestle for it," I said.

It was what Christine had said that night two years ago when I finally agreed that we should have a baby. When we were first dating, Christine and I agreed that we wanted to put off a family until we had gotten through graduate school, and were established in our jobs. Besides, we said, we were selfish. We wouldn't want to share each other with anybody else for a while.

But, soon after we were married, Christine began to raise the issue more often. She was studying for her M.A. exam in English, and would drop hints with literary references.

"Light in August?" she'd say. "Great Expectations?"

"In Our Time," I'd reply. "In Our Time."

We were living in our apartment above the print shop on the east side of town, and, although we actually had some money for a change, having paid off our college loans, we still hadn't bought a bed. Why did anyone have a bed? we wondered. It was just something to clean under.

Then, early one morning in May, dozing dreamily on our mattress on the floor, birds twirping furiously out the window, Christine turned to me with a smile, her hand tickling my stomach.

"Maybe we should buy a bed now," she said.

"Oh?" I said. "And why just now?"

She paused, a playful twist to her grin. "It might be hard for the pregnant lady of the house to get up off the floor in the morning."

Something like panic surged through my stomach, as I removed her hand. A mixture of nausea, betrayal, and rage. "What do you mean, pregnant?"

"Oh, I think so. I've missed two periods now. Isn't it great?"

"Wait a minute. I thought we hadn't decided about this yet."

She pulled back to her side of the mattress. "Yes, we did. 'In Our Time,' you said. I stopped taking the pill a few months ago."

"I didn't mean that our time was now," I said.

"That's not the way I heard it," she said, her eyes filling with tears as she threw off the covers and lurched into the bathroom.

"Obviously not," I tossed after her.

Had she really misunderstood? Or had she just hoped to trick me with a unilateral decision? And what was I supposed to do now? Be happy about it? Did I have any choice? For a week we barely spoke to each other, and, when we did, we fought.

—Did I want her to get an abortion?

—No.

—Did I think I wouldn't love the baby?

—Of course I would love the baby. That wasn't the point.

—Then what was the point?

—We hadn't agreed that this was the time.

—When exactly was the time?

—I didn't know, but the decision should have been mutual.

—When would I ever make such a decision?

—I didn't know if I had room in my life for another person.

—Maybe I didn't have room for her.

After two weeks of bickering I was ready to give in. If we were going to have a baby, I might as well try to be cheerful about it. I couldn't go on punishing her forever. And a baby would probably be good for both of us. I apologized, told her it was my fault, just my usual fear of

change. We bought an antique oak bed at a garage sale, installed a plywood base, and lugged our old mattress onto it. That night in bed, sexy and beaming, she turned to me.
"Let's not fight anymore," she said.
"Why not?" I said. "It's such fun."
"Okay, we could armwrestle for it," she said.
"For what?" I said.
"For whatever you want," she said.
"Right," I said, laughing.
"Hey, you think you can't beat me?" she said, as I let her pin me to the bed and have her way with me.

"What?" Goff said.
"Nothing," I said.
Goff seemed to be thinking. He had the look on his face that he always got right before he announced some plan to further insinuate himself into my life. He gazed off into the woods and then back down to my house. "I bet Fendelman'd take you on," he said. "I'd be willing to bet he would." He looked straight at me and raised his eyebrows as if he was actually serious. "It might make for some good entertainment."
"You're on," I hazarded, as if my parry had not been just a half-hearted joke.

And it wasn't. As it turned out, it was a precipitous challenge, and I have never been one to act precipitously. Or, as Christine was fond of insisting, I am useless in an emergency. It's funny how whole years can go by, important years, consigned, as it were, to oblivion, unmemorably, leaving no trace, while a few trivial seconds can impress themselves indelibly on the mind forever, expanding into huge, even monstrous proportions. Did Christine remember beating me at armwrestling? Did she remember the other things I did?

When Christine and I were first married, we got a kitten at the farmer's market. The first day we had it, it jumped up on a cheap metal bookcase and caught its paw under the rim of the top shelf. Terrified, hanging by one twisted paw, it shrieked and clambered, a dervish of fur and hisses. Closest to the bookcase, I froze. Somehow my brain just couldn't translate what I saw into action. Christine appeared almost instantaneously and freed the kitten before I had time to move. She looked at me with what could only have been astonishment.

"Why didn't you do something?" she said, and carried the kitten back to the bed, stroking and consoling it.

The flurry of fur and terror, the unanswered question, hung in the air for hours. And years later, the moment plagued me like it was yesterday. Somehow it seemed to reveal a major flaw in my character, an inability to act quickly, on impulse, to proceed without first patiently examining all sides of an issue.

Which is what I did when we bought our country property. We had a chance to buy the whole eighty acres at that time, but Christine was lukewarm to the idea, and it seemed like too much money to me. Rechecking our finances against the interest rates and down payments, and factoring in all the emergencies that might occur for which we would need money—the roof could go, the refrigerator break down, I might not get tenure—by the time I was ready to act, Goff had bought the forty-acre ridge for himself. Which was, in some ways, a relief to me. I knew we could afford the bottom forty acres with the barn and house, and Goff wouldn't do anything with the other forty but possibly log it off and farm it.

But now, with the prospect of Fendelman and his dynamite and drills, his rock crushers and trucks above us, I wished I'd just bought the whole parcel in the first place. So when Goff took my little joke about armwrestling seriously, I went with it. Without examining the possible repercussions, I acted as if I had meant it all along. Christine wasn't suitably impressed, I thought. She didn't perceive the immense character shift this required.

And now I was in Hansen's Bar in Ithaca, my hand clamped to Fendelman's over the battered formica table, my feet positioned stiffly on the black-and-white linoleum tile floor. Word had gotten out, and about a dozen people were there: Elmer Ernst, the town board chairman, who, along with Goff, had already quarried out the road to the west of my house; Ralph Pulvermacher, the largest man I'd ever met, and the one member of the town board who made an effort to get me some compensation for the loss of my spring; Ned Everman, the scrap metal dealer and junk artist who lived down in the hollow east of me; Stephanie, Goff's wife; and several of Goff's or Floyd's friends I didn't recognize. Even Christine was there—we had, after nearly a year-long separation prompted partly by our conflict over her false pregnancy and partly by her affair with Frank, been attempting a reconciliation—for moral support, though she thought the whole thing was a bit ridiculous. "It's like a tall tale," she said. "If it were in a book no one would believe it."

Goff had suggested two out of three falls, and he'd set the terms. If I won, he'd sell me the property opposite my house at a price I could pay. If Fendelman won, he'd sell it to Fendelman for considerably more. Goff was smiling wryly; it was a pretty safe bet. Fendelman was famous in the township for his armwrestling skill; he'd never been beaten. Tonight he had had quite a bit to drink and was more gregarious than usual, winking at Hansen, laughing at his friends' antics. "Haw!" he said as one of them pulled up a chair for me and beckoned daintily for me to sit down. Fendelman's arm was three times the size of mine, and my hand felt small and helpless in his hand.

Hansen tossed his bar rag on the counter and stood over us. "Okay, men," he said. "Feet flat on the floor, left hands in the air. Go on the count of three. *One* ..."

As he was nearing retirement, Willie Mays is reputed to have said, "I'll know it's time to quit when my brain says to my legs, 'Legs, go get that ball,' and my legs say, 'Who, me?'" Now every part of my body—my arms that had seen no heavier labor than hefting student papers in my briefcase, or wrestling with the assignments from my New Jersey textbook company; my legs that had rested beneath a library table and occasionally made their way around our farmyard behind the self-propelled mower; my stomach that had settled prematurely into the sag of middle age—was saying, "Who, me?"

Oh, I had tried to whip myself into shape for the event. I bought some free weights, did pushups, started running again. I'd lettered in cross-country in high school. I went out for the team as a sophomore partly because it seemed my best chance of getting a letter (and in 1959 if you didn't have a letter on your letter jacket you were a wimp) and partly because my father, once a semi-pro baseball player but now confined to a wheelchair with multiple sclerosis, seemed to want it.

"Give 'em hell," he'd say from his permanent installation in the living room. "Knock 'em dead for me."

The high school track team was coached by Raymond Schimmer, a tough, gnarly, white-haired man with a clipped way of speaking that incorporated a goad and a snarl. "Lean into it, Kingsley," he'd growl, as I rounded the mile-long practice field circle. "Stretch 'em out." His track team had won State ten years in a row, and he had a reputation for hounding prospective track men into going out for the team whether they wanted to or not. He'd call their fathers at the beginning of the season, as he'd called mine, and tell them that their sons could be All-State in shot put, 440, high hurdles—whatever he needed at the time. He didn't care as much about cross-country—it wasn't a "serious" sport—but he used it to scout prospective stars for his track team.

The first big race, held on a county golf course, with ten schools participating, terrified me. About a hundred-fifty runners milled around the starting line in their flimsy uniforms, slapping each other on the butts, laughing, pumping each other up. I had no idea which way the course went, but figured I'd have lots of guys to follow.

At the gun I was submerged in a mass of spikes flashing, bodies bobbing all around me. Very quickly I lost sight of my teammates, and, not knowing what pace to set, ran as hard as I could. Collapsed on the finish line, Coach Schimmer yelling at me to get up and walk it off, I saw Jerry Jeffers, the star of the team, come in a full minute behind me. Jeffers was stunned. How could I, a mere sophomore, in my first meet, have beaten him?

But he wasn't as stunned as I was. I knew I shouldn't have beaten him, and I'd never beat him again.

My father encouraged me. "You beat him once," my father said. "Don't think about it too much, just run."

And I did manage to keep pace for a few races, coming in only seconds behind him. Then, about mid-season my father contracted a pulmonary infection, and, weakened by the multiple sclerosis, nearly died before Thanksgiving.

It wasn't that I deliberately slowed down; I don't think it was just my father's condition that did it. It was a different kind of mental block. The fact of my beating Jerry Jeffers just didn't jibe with my conviction that I wasn't that good. Somehow my body adjusted its capabilities to fit my will. I didn't have the killer instinct.

Coach Schimmer did his best to browbeat me, threatening in his ignorance to call my father. "Run through that pain, Kingsley," he'd yell at me, misperceiving my stoniness. But I'd ignore him. Some kinds of pain you just don't run through.

At the beginning of the season Coach Schimmer had said seven of the fourteen men on the team would get letters. At the end of the season I finished seventh. Despite Coach Schimmer's impassioned calls to my mother, I didn't go out for track that year or cross-country the next.

But faced now with Fendelman, I remembered Jerry Jeffers. As my father said, I had beaten Jeffers when by all rights I shouldn't have. Maybe I could beat Fendelman. I had read news stories about fathers who had lifted automobiles to free their trapped infant sons. Anything was possible.

"*Two* ..." Hansen said.

Fendelman's arm went rigid, his muscles bulging from his T-shirt. He closed his grip on my hand, crushing my knuckles together. I wondered what Christine was thinking. Things hadn't worked out with Frank in Milwaukee, country life now seemed more attractive to her, and we had been together again for the past several months. We had talked about what we might do if we were able to buy Goff's parcel. She had an idea about milk goats and cheese, and, though I wondered where we'd get water and what we'd do in the winter, the idea appealed to me. She also had an idea about kids of another variety. "The Son Also Rises?" she said.

We both agreed that, if a quarry went in, we'd cut our losses and move back to town, something I didn't want to do. The farm seemed a reasonable substitute for a family. Over the past few months, working on prairie restoration and gardening, we seemed to be coming to a better understanding about our lives together.

"*Th—*"

Fendelman slammed my hand to the table as a whoop went up from the crowd.

"*—ree!*" said Hansen.

"Haw!" Fendelman said.

"One fall," Hansen said. "You boys want a rest?"

"Naw," Fendelman said.

We clasped hands again, and Hansen began his count. This time I was quicker, our hands quavering upright in an isometric standoff before the count of two. And then, Fendelman began to weaken. Imperceptibly at first, then visibly, I began to bend his arm back, the crowd laughing and hollering at Fendelman who looked like a cartoon. His eyes were squinted, his brow knit, his temples bulging, his cheeks popped out, his large face red with effort. His whole body quavered, his attention focusing on our hands in concentrated disbelief.

    I had him halfway from the table. And then Fendelman looked up and smiled stupidly.

    "Oh, my gawrsh," Fendelman drawled, exaggeratedly. "He's got me now. Whut a He-Man. I guess I better just give up now. Whew! He's got the strength of ten men, or one-tenth of a man. Haw!"

    Fendelman was playing with me. He could slam my hand back any time he wanted. Defeated, I stopped pushing. The sudden unexpected release of tension took Fendelman by surprise, and our hands suddenly swung to my side of the table. For a split second Fendelman relaxed, confused, and at that precise moment I slammed down with all the strength I could muster. Fendelman's hand was flat on the table, his face pinched in a frown.

    "Whuh?" he said.

    "Hey, Fendelman," jeered one of his friends. "The city slicker too tough for you?"

    A small ripple of laughter went up, but subsided quickly to silence, as Fendelman leaned forward, determined.

    "Shut up," he said. "Come on, shithead, third fall. Now."

    Hansen wasted no time with his count, and we both anticipated "three" at somewhere well before "one." Our hands held vertical for ten seconds, twenty, thirty. My shoulder stabbed with pain, and my whole hand, knuckles rippling beneath Fendelman's large grip like brittle sticks, cracked and split. And then I saw what he had in mind. He wasn't going to beat me right away. He was going to break my hand first.

It was as if a bright searing light had exploded in my bones—the spatter of deep-fried fat, an electric jolt, lightning—and my grasp collapsed. And that was that. Fendelman got up without a word, grabbed a pitcher of beer, and went out into the night.

Hansen ambled back behind the bar, and the crowd, a nervous murmur of concern, dispersed. My arm was still flat on the table, immobile, loquacious with pain.

"You been beat, boy," said Goff gravely. "Still, in ten years I don't recall Fendelman ever having to go to the third fall. I guess that's something."

My hand was in a cast for six weeks, and it has never been quite the same. Sometimes when I forget and put weight on it at night, half asleep, the pain is enough to make me cry out. But Goff didn't sell the land to Fendelman after all. Goff thought it was unsportsmanlike of Fendelman to break my hand—it actually angered him—and he made us a counterproposal instead. He'd sell us the land at our price and then we'd lease it (and our other pasture land) back to him for a dollar a year for ten years. That way, we would own the land and pay the taxes and protect our interests, but he would have the use of it. It was an offer we couldn't refuse, he said. He agreed to do no more than he always had, cutting some firewood and pasturing his cows. There would be no quarry, but no goat farm either.

Christine was kind of proud of me, I think. The summer seemed to have changed things between us, and we imagined growing old and fat together. When she began once again to suggest that we think about children, I thought it was not a bad idea. I thought it was something to think on.

skin

"This might sound strange," she says, "but I'm sort of worried about how we'll pay for the plastic surgery when I lose all that weight."

"Plastic surgery?" I say. We're walking along the beach at Mazomanie—inching along, really. At five-feet-two and two hundred pounds—and with her ankle, foot, and knee problems—she can't move very fast, the August sun melting her buttery face. Discreetly behind my sunglasses, I'm eyeing the thong bikinis, the fleshy tremolo of twenty-something centerfolds strutting their stuff around us.

"Well," she says, "I think about all that skin, empty of fat." She says she heard of a man who actually sold his excess skin to a medical supply company to help pay for the cosmetic treatments.

"No," I say. "That's ridiculous. It doesn't work that way. You might have a few wrinkles, but the skin shrinks *skin*

as you lose weight. It's not like emptying a plastic grocery sack."

In all our months of talking about her weight—how she's going to lose it; how I like her fat; how thin is just a cultural affectation, a stinginess, a lack—we've never had this particular conversation. But then, she's always coming up with these oddball speculations—how one of her friends at Weight Watchers was pregnant with twins and didn't know it until one day they just popped out; how she read of a man whose fat caught fire like tallow in a saucepan. And so, even though it's crazy, I'm thinking about her skin splayed out like a huge hot air balloon, deflated, a thin loopy membrane of silk.

"Are you sure?" she says.

I roll my eyes and sigh as two tanned, oily haunches divided by a lone black thread pass us by. I try to imagine her in that body, trailing a billow of skin, the thin Mylar housing flapping, abandoned.

She takes my hand and I snap back, her sausagey fingers fueling my usual hunger.

"Hang on to your skin," I say, as we float slowly along toward a future that threatens to thin all around us. "Hang on to your skin." And I hold on to her like a gondola holds on to a dirigible. And the turning world stares up at us, with envy and with wonder.

a *trick* of *memory*

"there are some things you learn to do when you start getting fat," Wilford said. He stretched back at the picnic table, his hands straight at his sides gripping the seat as he looked out over the lake. "For one thing you always find yourself a big enough chair." He patted the picnic bench. "I once sat down in one of those little white metal chairs, the kind you get at K-Mart for five bucks? And when I went to stand up, the chair stuck to me." Wilford laughed, a short, cheerful laugh, somewhere between a chortle and a snort. He removed his thick wire-rimmed glasses and wiped the sweat from around his eyes with his thumb and forefinger. His teeth protruded behind his lips, giving his face a swollen, cartoon flair, as if his cheeks were full of cotton balls. "Actually, it was kind of funny, so I did it again the next time I was at a party."

Peterson's two aunts laughed, and dragged on their cigarettes, blowing the smoke aslant out of the sides of their mouths. They looked younger than Peterson had imagined they would when he was describing them for Christine in the car on the way to the resort. Martha, the youngest, looked more like forty-seven than fifty-seven; Ida seemed nowhere near seventy; and his uncle Wilford seemed too boyish to have just retired from his house painting business in Ames, Iowa.

They had gathered at Pine Lake, Wisconsin, over the Fourth of July weekend for the reunion. Peterson hadn't seen Wilford since he was a kid. He remembered riding behind Wilford's wife Evelyn's horse on her father's farm near Independence when he was perhaps twelve, as she broke into a gallop and he slid down the horse's rump where he was sure he would fall off or get kicked. They rode around the pasture for what seemed like hours, Wilford laughing as they passed him, "Look at Petey. He sure is having fun."

Now Wilford was continuing his monologue. "Or you start wearing ties. I never wore ties until I put on weight, but the collar hides your neck's unsightly flaps and folds, or gives the *illusion,*" he paused over the word "illusion" as if caressing it, "the illusion that you still have a neck. And the vertical line draws attention away from your gut." Wilford spoke slowly and laconically, with a slight drawl. "Of course the real joke," he laughed again, a slow snort through his nose like someone with a chronic sinus condition, "is when your gut hangs out over your belt. I was painting a house last summer—the Varden place, you remember, Evie?"

Evelyn nodded, and rolled her eyes. Sitting in a lawn

chair slightly to one side of the group, she was so quiet you could forget she was there. Wilford seemed to use her as a prop for his stories, a kind of punctuation mark or device of pacing. Peterson remembered her slim legs and hips in her tight western jeans, her cowboy hat and boots, the white broadcloth shirt she wore when he clung to her waist, his hands tight around her stomach on the back of the horse. Now she was fifty-eight, frail and bony, with an enigmatic grin and eyes that seemed to look off in the distance.

"I had on my khaki painting pants," Wilford continued. "I had on my khakis without the belt, and when I reached up on the ladder to get the eaves, the damn pants fell to my knees. Old Mrs. Varden had a conniption fit, laughing." Wilford chuckled through his nose, his thick cheeks inflating. "Suspenders help."

Ida laughed. It was an abrupt brittle laugh mingled with cigarette smoke. "Wilford used to be a stick—as skinny as you are, Peterson, or Evelyn."

"And good-looking," Martha said. "He could have had his pick of the girls, but Evelyn got him."

"I remember," Peterson said. "I remember watching Wilford play center field for that minor league team in Elm Grove. He was fast."

"Times change," Wilford said. "You got to compensate."

"That's not so easy," Ida said, straightening up, her black halter top flat against her dark skin. She was what you would call "gaunt," Peterson thought, a combination of age, smoking, bourbon, and nerves. Her husband, Albert, who had owned a taxidermy shop in Des Moines, had been a bull of a man, and a heavy drinker. He had taken Peterson fishing years ago in Minnesota and boasted of "taxidermying Japs" during the war. He had more than once put his fist through the wall of their living room. Ida started drinking, too, and now that Albert was gone she still drank heavily, ate little, and stayed thin. "I wouldn't mind putting on a little weight," she said. "What's your secret?"

"You can have some of mine," Martha said. She pulled one foot up under her on the picnic bench and smiled girlishly. "All I have to do is look at food."

Peterson wondered why Martha had never married. She was a little chubby, but even at fifty-seven she was cute and sweet. She had a softness about her that Peterson had always liked in a woman, that you didn't see much anymore. Christine had had that softness when they first met, but recently she had been dieting. Now, she seemed all angles and edges.

Martha stubbed her cigarette out in her Diet Pepsi can. "If I'm not eating, I'm smoking." Her laughter shimmered in the heavy air. She always seemed to have some boyfriend or other, Peterson remembered, but she had a way of attracting losers—shoe salesmen down on their luck, liquor store clerks, unemployed factory workers. The fact that a man wanted her seemed reason enough to want him.

Wilford turned to Ida. "Oh, you don't want any of this," he said, grabbing a fistful of fat. "This only looks good on a man."

"You know, it's interesting," Christine was saying, "how people will pack up and come *here* for a whole week. I mean, this place is right on the road, the cabins are in disrepair, the lake is just a lake with resorts all around it. Yet people will drive hundreds of miles for this. I guess it has to do with a way of life."

"It's what my family did when I was a kid," Peterson said.

"Yes, yes. But if you and I were going to stay at a cabin on a lake, we'd want something in a national park or national forest—something secluded and beautiful."

She had a point, Peterson thought. Pine Haven Resort and Campground was indeed on the road, though it was not a particularly busy road. On one side a large neon sign announced CAMPING, but the campground was little more than a pull-off with a few grassy spots on a gravel loop that paralleled the road. At the end of the "campground" was a new, homemade miniature golf concession. The resort itself, on the other side of the road by the lake, consisted only of a snack bar, a fish cleaning house, and eleven rustic cabins.

"It's a whole way of life," Christine continued cheerfully. "I mean, these people work fifty-one weeks a year at some low-paying job, and then come here for their one-week vacation?" She gestured around the cabin, which was old, paneled in knotty pine. There was a small hole in the linoleum floor under the formica table where the boards had rotted through. In one corner a driftwood lamp partially blocked the doorway into the bedroom, which was furnished only with a built-in bed and shelves. It made Peterson nostalgic for the Minnesota resorts where his family had vacationed years ago, before his father died and his mother married Eddie and moved to Arizona. The summers he had spent fishing and swimming and boating at the lake had been among the happiest in his life, he thought. Or perhaps that was just a trick of memory.

"You know, there's a national forest not far from here, fifteen miles maybe—Chequamegon," Christine was saying. "We could drive up there for an hour and hike. Unless you'd rather sit around here. I mean, it's your reunion, so you should do what you want to. I mean, it would be fine with me if you want to stay here. Really. But I'm going to drive up there."

Peterson hesitated, as she waited for his answer. He knew what she wanted him to say, and he knew what she meant about the resort. It wasn't a particularly attractive place. It was certainly more run-down than they had expected, and the clientele seemed clearly working class. Having leased their country place to Goff and moved back to town, they were doing pretty well and didn't have to stay in a place like this. Peterson was teaching history at the college, and Christine, who had worked for him at his print shop while she completed her M.A., now was working part-time at the Department of Social Services.

Peterson knew what she meant, but something in her cheerful tone annoyed him. It wasn't that it was superior exactly, though that was part of it. Her father had been a respected physician in their small town, and she valued the prestige. But more, it was that she was so confident about what was good and what wasn't. She had a way of imposing her values and preferences on everyone else. Her idea of a proper vacation was the month-long car trips through the West her family had taken when she was young. They stayed in the best hotels and motels along the way, and visited every national park and monument. They had "educational experiences." When they got back home, they joked that they had to "rest up" by going back to work.

"You coming or not?" Christine said.

They stopped at a grocery in Pinewood, a one-street town that existed solely for the tourists. There was a bar with a paisley hearse parked out front, a run-down bait shop, a sandwich place called "The Eat Inn," and a restaurant with pretenses, "The Pinewood." The grocery was a wood frame building with an antique storefront and a sign that said merely, "The Store."

The Store was full of the kind of stuff Peterson had, as a child, found intriguing: slip bobbers, fish hats, hand-carved wooden animals, grab bags, T-shirts, key chains, little doohickeys for the tackle box and shop. The floors were worn wooden planks, and one counter, filled with penny candies and old postcards, smacked of the nineteenth century. Peterson browsed the aisle labeled with a hand-painted sign, TRASH OR TREASURE, while Christine shopped for dinner. He'd told her that he'd be catching fish, but she insisted they have something on hand, "just in case." When he was young, Peterson recalled, and his father could still go out in the boat, his mother always waited for them and dinner. If they caught nothing, they all went out to the drive-in.

Peterson joined Christine at the cereals and popped a large box of Sugar Smacks into the cart.

"Don't buy that crap," she said, her voice a mixture of weariness and accusation.

"What?"

"It's not good for you." She took the box out and placed it back on the shelf. "How about something else? Something we can *both* eat."

Peterson stared at her. "I don't want something else."

"You know how I feel about this. When you eat that stuff, you don't eat anything good." She smiled, but there was a hard edge to the smile. "And anyway, you might get fat." She poked Peterson in the stomach. It was an effort at pleasantry, but it coiled in his gut.

"Look," he said. "You buy your coffee. I don't like coffee. It's not particularly good for you. But I don't complain about your coffee."

"Do you want me to stop drinking coffee?"

"That's not the point."

"Yes, it is. I want you to stop eating crap. When are you going to get your cholesterol tested again, by the way? You promised that when this summer …"

"Sugar Smacks doesn't have any cholesterol," he said.

"You didn't want to come with me today from the start, did you? I told you it was fine with me if you didn't want to come, so why did you come?"

"I thought you wanted me to."

"It's not my problem. You've got to learn to say what you want. You want to go back, I'll take you back. I'll go on alone."

Peterson glared at the ceiling. "Jesus," he said. "What are you anyway, my mother?"

"What are you, my child?" she called after him as he wheeled cockeyed down the aisle.

When they met again at the checkout, Peterson watched the clerk tally up the taco mix, frozen hamburger, tomatoes, lettuce, cheese, and coffee.

"Look, this is stupid," he said.

"Yes, it is," she said, a certain musical lilt to her voice.

"Let's start over."

"Okay," she said. "I'll drive."

The drive was longer than Peterson had anticipated. He hadn't checked the map, and the fifteen miles stretched into more like fifty, the hour into two. The road to the park was under construction and barricaded, but Christine drove on anyway. Because of the holiday, the heavy equipment was idle as the car bumped over potholes and rubble, sending clouds of dust out over the yellow Caterpillars and road graders that hunkered on the roadside. Sweat dripped from Peterson's forehead, his foot pressing an imaginary brake pedal to the floor as they lurched along the deserted roadbed. His father had always driven the car on trips. Even when the multiple sclerosis put him in a wheelchair, he had hand controls installed in the '54 Ford, and he continued to drive. Now, sitting in the passenger seat, Peterson felt somehow naked, and powerless.

"It's pretty here," he said when they had pulled off the road at a trailhead. "Sure will be nice when they get the road finished." *You lied to me,* he added silently. *You said fifteen miles.*

They hiked several miles on an unmaintained trail through brambles and prickly ash to a small lake, sweat beading on Peterson's forehead, an army of black flies strafing him. Christine plunged ahead as if indifferent to the condition of the trail, while Peterson waved his arms wildly.

"Isn't it nice?" she sighed when they arrived at the lake. "So isolated and quiet."

When they finally got back to the car, she immediately went for the driver's side. "If you don't mind," she said.

Back at the resort, Christine made straight for the picnic table, where Wilford was again holding court, and

Peterson headed for the pool to cool off. Looking back he could see Christine talking animatedly, no doubt concocting, he thought, some glowing account of the abortive trip.

Peterson's mother was in the pool, leaning against the edge in the deep end, tossing a ball to one of Peterson's second cousins. There were five or six of them around, all the same age, and Peterson couldn't seem to get them straight. He bought a Snickers bar at the counter and slid into the water beside her, gazing off at the Heilman's sign over the snack bar. It was a small pool—it would have fit neatly in their own backyard—but it was welcome. The resort had no beach, and the lake was weedy.

The ball bounced across the water, splashing Peterson in the face, and his mother tossed it back as Amy or Sabrina or Jessica chased after it.

"Did you have a nice drive?" she asked. Her brown hair was bleached and frizzy, cut short in a crooked mop for the summer. Except for the little vertical lines around her mouth, and the abundance of freckles or age spots, Peterson thought she had changed little over the years. She had always been one of the youngest mothers among his friends', and that pleased him for some reason.

"We had a fight," he said. The ball smashed into the water inches from Peterson's face. He tossed it back.

His mother didn't seem particularly interested or surprised. Perhaps it made her uncomfortable. "Are you having more of these lately?" She waved and smiled at Stacey or Sybil who was getting out of the pool.

Peterson began to present his side of the story, but stopped short. He had never mentioned their fights to anyone. He'd always suspected that his mother secretly liked Christine better than him. She loved him as a mother would, of course, but from the day he'd introduced Christine to her some years ago, they'd seemed to have endless things to talk about. They'd disappear into the kitchen and talk for hours while Peterson watched TV or read a book. His mother hadn't changed much physically, Peterson thought, but his father's illness had forced her to become stronger and more independent. Maybe that was what she liked in Christine—her strength and independence.

"So what have you been doing all afternoon?" he said.

When Peterson left his mother at the pool, his uncle and his two aunts were still at the picnic table, but Christine had left. Wilford was describing the boat he'd bought for his retirement.

"When I brought that boat home—" Wilford said, "got the whole thing, boat, motor, hitch, and trailer, for three-hundred bucks—when I brought that boat home, Evie said, 'what the hell are you going to do with that?' Well, it *is* the middle of Iowa, and we don't have lakes like this," he gestured toward the water where a speedboat cruised by towing a skier. "But we got these farmers' ponds, see, and there's this one that's more like a lake than a pond, and I said I was thinking of getting into fishing. She's mainly sore that I didn't work another year or two and took early retirement. Now she has to keep working, for the benefits. Isn't that right, Evie?"

He paused while everyone looked at Evelyn. She smiled, but it seemed a sour smile, just a slight twist to her lip or a nearly imperceptible roll of the eyes that no one but Peterson seemed to notice.

"And you know what?" Wilford continued. "I took

some buddies out in that boat and caught the goddamndest (pardon my language) big catfish you ever saw—first time I'd been fishing in twenty years. Between the weight of that fish and me we nearly sunk the boat." Wilford paused, the memory of the fish swelling his lips. The roar of the speedboat caromed off the pine trees as harpsichord music floated improbably from someone's boom box.

"Fat chance," Evelyn said quietly.

Wilford sat up suddenly and pointed under the cabin. "What's that?" he said. "A snake big as my arm just went under your cabin, Martha. A rattler, I bet."

Martha slid quickly out from the picnic table. "I don't like snakes," she said.

Ida and Evelyn gathered their cigarette cases and towels and eased back from the table.

"Whoa!" Wilford said. "Looks like it's headed for the bathroom drainpipe—maybe it's got a nest in there. Look, it's going up the pipe."

It was dark under the cabin, but among the loose boards, pieces of Styrofoam minnow buckets, and old wire and glass, Peterson thought he could see a snake—tan, patterned with black. Or maybe it was a piece of rope.

"I'm going to tell the manager," Ida said. "We don't want snakes in our cabin." She shuddered dramatically. "Come on, Martha, Evelyn."

"We'll stay and keep an eye on it," Wilford said, as the three women retreated toward the lodge.

"Was that really a rattlesnake?" Peterson asked when they were gone.

"Naw," Wilford said. "I was just tired of the women. It works every time. Probably just a pine snake, or a water snake. If it is a snake. Harmless."

Peterson stared at the cabin as Wilford tugged at his jaw.

"You having some conflict with the missus?" Wilford asked. "She's a little firebrand, she is."

"Not really," Peterson said.

"You know what your problem is? You're too uptight. You got to lighten up," Wilford said. "That tall and silent crap just doesn't cut it anymore." Much of the drawl had left his voice, and he spoke slightly faster, with more intensity. "You ain't, for Christ sake, no goddamn John Wayne. You got to talk 'em to death. Talk is what they respect and understand." His face seemed to have thinned some, the cotton gone out of his cheeks. "Talk 'em to death, and throw some weight around, or they'll get you by the balls." He gazed out at the lake where a loon had broken into shrill, lyrical laughter.

"Thanks for the advice," Peterson said.

Wilford laughed slowly through his nose. "Sure is a nice quiet place here," he drawled.

Back at the cabin, Christine was fixing dinner. Peterson hadn't caught any fish that morning, and hadn't gotten around to fishing again in the afternoon. The smell of horseradish and Tabasco was in the air.

"Going fishing this evening?" Christine asked cheerfully, though it rankled like a slap.

Peterson sat down at the table, bowls of tomato, lettuce, and shredded cheese neatly arranged on the plastic red-checkered tablecloth with its centerpiece of chicory, daisies, and Queen Anne's lace. He wasn't particularly hungry. The candy bar had filled him up, and his stomach bulged slightly over the elastic band of the swimming suit he had had since college. Maybe he was putting on a little weight himself.

He leaned back in his chair and gazed out the cabin window at the lake, Christine busy in the kitchenette behind him. "You know," he said, his voice slow and steady, "Wilford and I saw a snake under our cabin. He thinks maybe it's a rattlesnake, maybe it's got a nest under there."

The coffeepot hissed on the stove, as Christine lifted it off the burner.

"A rattlesnake?" she said. "Don't be ridiculous. He's just putting you on. It must have been a water snake, or a pine snake. There isn't a rattlesnake within a hundred miles of here."

yogurt

They were fighting more than usual lately, or perhaps fighting had just become usual, he thought, as they walked home from Yogurt Express along the dark side street. There was no moon, and in the darkness the houses loomed huge and unfamiliar.

He was thinking about earlier in the week, at the family reunion, when they'd fought over the sugar cereal. He'd tossed it into the cart, and she'd taken it out, reprimanding him.

"I don't want you buying this crap," she'd said.

"Jesus," he'd replied, wheeling off cockeyed down the aisle. "What are you anyway, my mother?"

These petty clashes rankled him more and more, and he held onto them for days, replaying every nuance and detail, running his mind over them like a tongue on a sore tooth.

yogurt

Now, as they walked along the quiet street, not touching, he thought what it would be like to live alone again, all that freedom. The idea of a separation—he with his own space, his own time, his own decisions—increasingly gave him pleasure. There were, of course, the complications of the house, the new car, the bank account, the real estate, but was that any reason to stay together?

A rapid slap of feet on pavement just behind them brought him up short, and, as he turned, startled, a cup of cold yogurt slashed into his face, blinding him.

"Hey!" he shouted.

A dark shape scurried past, turning the corner. "I hate couples!" it snarled, and disappeared.

He felt weak, his breath uneven. "What was *that?*" he said, wiping yogurt from his eyes and chin.

She was silent a moment, and then, "I've seen him before," she said. "In the daytime. He wears a skullcap and sort of slinks around. I thought he was harmless."

"Jesus, it's such a ... a ..."

"Violation?" She gave him the word he was looking for.

"Yes, a violation. I wonder if we should report him. Warn the neighbors. Lock our doors."

They had reached the corner, but no one was there. In the light of the streetlamp, she looked serene, and, he thought, well, *valuable*. He put his arm around her and drew her close. Slowly, she put her arm around him.

the new sidewalks

Peterson had been forgetting things. Not just people's names or little things that everybody forgot sometimes. He had been forgetting things that were second nature, things so much a part of him that he shouldn't have had to remember them at all.

Last week, when he got in the car to drive to the mall he couldn't remember where the headlight switch was. He sat there in the dark, staring at the shadowy dash and gripping the ridged steering wheel. It was a bitterly cold night; the hazy moon cast an eerie light out over the neighborhood, causing the new sidewalks to glow.

The sidewalks had been replaced the previous summer, because they had come up for replacement on the city's schedule. The old sidewalks had been poured back when cement was mostly granite and stone, and they were an attractive pinkish-gray color. He received a notice in

the new sidewalks

the mail that his "hazardous and defective" sidewalks would be replaced at a cost of one hundred dollars per slab, payable upon completion.

When he went out to check his walk, he found that someone had been through the neighborhood already marking slabs for replacement. A few of his slabs were feathered at the edges or had small hairline cracks. One had settled slightly over the years. He was sure they would all easily last another fifty years. But each slab was spray-painted with arrows, indicating that they would all be replaced. The sidewalks in the next block were only a year old, and already pocked and deteriorating after one Wisconsin winter.

He called to protest. The supervisor explained how, with the new methods of laying cement, you couldn't replace a single slab—the new cement expanded and contracted differently than the old. If you put them side by side the old cement would crack the new. Therefore, although only one or two slabs might actually be defective, the city would have to replace them all. Still, if Peterson liked, he could send the inspector over.

The inspector came that afternoon.

"You're right," the inspector said. He was a small, fat man, who puffed as he walked, and continually wiped sweat from his forehead with a large dirty handkerchief. "There's nothing wrong with most of these slabs. But this one," he hit the slab with his pointer, "has settled a good inch below the others. A senior citizen could come along and trip and sue the city for a million bucks. Anyway, the work is scheduled. Your neighbors want these walks replaced. You wouldn't stand in their way, now would you?"

Peterson talked with the neighbors. Some were indifferent and some shared his outrage, but nothing finally came of it. They had lives and jobs and weren't prepared to devote any time to stopping "progress." "You can't fight city hall," they said.

Peterson remembered all this vividly. And he remembered Christine's disinterest. "There are more important things to worry about," she said. "Like your daughter. But then you're not here to listen to her cry all day."

He was there to hear her cry all night, but he figured that was just what babies did. They cried. He could sleep through it. Christine couldn't. Things hadn't been going so well since Jennifer was born last year. It seemed like he and Christine no longer had any time together to talk.

Now he sat in the car staring at the shadowy dash, panicked. He couldn't remember where the headlight switch was. He pulled a stalk to the right of the steering wheel; the windshield wipers swept across the dry windshield in their mocking syncopated rhythm. He flipped another stalk and the turn indicator click-clacked at him. He tried not to think, just let his body find the lights instinctively. The lights came on.

He had for some time felt that he was losing control of these simple things; the world he had accepted in its order and logic had begun to seem strange, arbitrary, and alien. It often happened when he was driving. He would be traveling some familiar route, shopping for the baby, or visiting a friend, when suddenly he'd be lost. Suddenly nothing looked familiar at all. It was as if he were in a strange city, with no recognizable landmarks. He would try to visualize the route he had taken countless times, and couldn't. He would feel a whelming sense of panic, and

then recover his equilibrium and remember.
He supposed there were explanations. He was distracted by problems at home or at school. He wasn't paying attention. But there were other things. He remembered years ago his parents' friends solemnly declaring, "I never forget a face." It seemed an odd boast at the time. Who could forget a face? It wasn't even a matter of memory, he thought. You saw someone once, you just naturally recognized them when you saw them again. But recently he had been forgetting faces. He would meet people at parties who seemed to know all about him, had had, it appeared, conversations with him. He strained to remember who they were, how he might have known them. But they seemed like strangers.

It was happening with his students, too. They would greet him in the halls, or come to his office for a conference, and he wouldn't know who they were. Had they been in before? Was he repeating himself? He listened carefully for clues.

"Hi, Professor," they'd say.

"Hey, friend," he'd respond. He'd taken to calling everyone "friend" to avoid either names or neutrality.

"Well, here I am."

"Yes, you are."

"Well?"

"Well what?"

"What did you think?"

"I'm sorry. I seem to have forgotten ..."

"About the paper."

"Ah, yes. The paper. I've just read through fifty papers. Yours was the one about ..."

"The New Deal."

"Yes, of course. Let's see. I've just got it here."

Often he didn't remember reading the paper at all. He'd stare at the erasable bond, smeared where his hand had sweated as he wrote out comments. He wrote elaborate comments, and, using them as an outline, he'd deliver a short lecture. It usually worked. The students would go away, satisfied, leaving him in his office wondering if he was losing his mind. How could a history teacher function without a memory?

Sometimes he would find himself in the middle of a lecture he had given numerous times before, when suddenly he would begin to doubt his own words. Things he had known without question, things everybody knew, suddenly seemed doubtful. "Harry S. Truman," he'd hear himself say, and then stop. Was "S" his middle initial? Maybe it was "F." Maybe it wasn't even Truman. In the silence it seemed that the students were mocking him. They stared up, pencils poised.

But here it was, written in his lecture notes, the same lecture he'd given last year. It must be true. He had taken to writing all his lectures down, word for word, to avoid embarrassment if he forgot things. It seemed to work. His students always gave him enthusiastic course evaluations. He got some of the highest marks in the department. But he felt like history was erasing itself all around him. How long could he keep up the ruse?

The car was beginning to warm up as he drove. He was going to meet Christine at the Red Lobster. She had spent the day at her mother's; she was spending more and more time there. Her mother was more sympathetic about the baby's crying than Peterson, although she often thought Jennifer was just hungry. "Are you sure she's getting enough milk?" she'd say.

This evening Christine was leaving Jennifer with her mother and would meet Peterson at the restaurant. He had gone to the medical library earlier to look up Alzheimer's, and then he had been to see his doctor. The library hadn't been much help. It seemed everybody had Alzheimer's these days, and the major sources at the library were checked out. At least he had an appointment with the doctor.

Dr. Reich was a small boyish fellow who appeared irritated that Peterson was there. "What seems to be the trouble?" he asked.

Peterson told him.

The doctor poked and prodded, took urine samples and blood, and said he'd call in a week. "You seem to be in good health," he said. "Are you under a lot of stress? Stress can cause memory loss." Dr. Reich advised Peterson to cut back on aspirin and caffeine. "Sometimes even bad weather can affect our mental health," he said. "Of course, it could be something neurological." He threw the possibility out like a sop, and Peterson grabbed it.

Peterson's own father had been an invalid all his life, and Peterson had always had a sharper sense of mortality than most people, he thought. Even as a small child he had spent hours lying awake at night, brooding about suicide and death, thinking about his father's paralysis, his wheelchair, his catheter sacks and lifts. People were so fragile. So much could go wrong. You had no control over anything. Maybe that was why he liked history. It seemed fixed and dependable and unchanging.

When he arrived at the restaurant, Christine was already in a booth. The two menus were atop each other in the middle of the table, and Christine was staring straight ahead. She looked tired. She probably didn't want to hear about his talk with the doctor, or his recent bout with forgetting. He had expressed his worries before, and she had dismissed them. She forgot things, too, she said. So did everybody. He was hypersensitive. No, he'd think of something happier to tell her.

Then he saw she was crying. He sat down, searching his memory. Had he forgotten something? "What is it?" he asked.

"The doctor," she sobbed.

He had forgotten that she was taking the baby to the doctor today. She was worried about Jennifer's crying.

"Jennifer's head isn't growing," she said.

"What?" Peterson said. "What do you mean?"

"Her head hasn't grown in three months. She's fallen off the bottom of the growth charts. The sutures are closed. She's going to be retarded."

Peterson didn't know what to say. "There must be some mistake." He took her hand across the table.

"What would you know about it?" she said.

Late that night, his wife in bed and finally sleeping, the baby whimpering in her crib, Peterson left the house. The night was clear and cold, the ice on the sidewalks crunching with every step in a pleasant repetitive rhythm. The streetlamps glowed cold over the neighborhood, the lights in the houses out.

He walked to the end of the block, his whole body numbed by the cold, and then to the end of the next one.

the new sidewalks

Somewhere far off a semi shifted down on the beltline with somewhere to go; a dog howled at the new moon.

The cold and the loneliness were soothing as Peterson watched his feet walk from block to block. He could see now why they needed to replace the concrete, how just one cracked or unsettled slab could throw the whole sidewalk off. Now the new sidewalks stretched white and perfect beyond him into the comforting dark.

He walked. And as he walked he thought he remembered something that he wanted to tell Christine, something important, something that would make them all happy. But no, he had forgot.

the sacred well

She was leaning forward in the seat again, exaggeratedly enunciating questions for the driver. "What are those birds called? How much money does the average Mexican make? What is the economy based on?" It set Peterson's teeth on edge. Why did she have to be the loud American, smiling so fatuously in her good-humored, unself-conscious ignorance? And yet he found himself interested in the answers, too, as Christine made notations in her little book, and Carlos, the driver, patiently played tour guide in his best broken English.

They had been in Mexico for three days, having left Jennifer with Christine's mother. The trip had been Christine's idea. Nearly everything they did was her idea. Peterson would have preferred just to stay home where things were familiar and to try to read his books and prepare his classes over the Christmas vacation. But Christine had insisted that they needed the change. It had been nearly nine months now since their year-old daughter had been diagnosed as microcephalic. Her head wasn't growing; she had fallen off the bottom of the growth charts and would almost certainly be retarded. Jennifer cried twenty-four hours a day, and Peterson, despite his efforts to love her, had visions of picking her up by her tiny feet, whirling her around his head, and slamming her into the wall. He was angry, distraught, heartbroken. They would have to put her into an institution. They could not handle her at home.

The trip seemed doomed from the outset. The plane to Florida was two hours late arriving in Chicago—a splintered windshield. While the flight attendant joked about it over the intercom, Peterson half hoped that they would miss their Miami connection. When they arrived in Miami, minutes before the flight to Merida was scheduled to leave from the other end of the airport, two miles away, Peterson was ready to turn around. But when Christine grabbed his duffel bag along with her own and began running through the terminal, he had no choice but to follow her. Arriving at the tram, he found her already on it, her foot wedged in the door for him, warning buzzers sounding, and airport officials angrily insisting that she let the door close.

They arrived at the gate just as the boarding platform was being removed, and Christine managed to persuade the attendants at the desk to delay the flight long enough for them to board. When the plane landed in Cozumel for a brief stopover, the pilot nearly missed the runway, apparently underestimating the approach and screeching to a prolonged and terrifying stop with the wheels off the concrete and the nose of the plane protruding into the jungle. Everyone on the plane applauded.

 In Merida the hotel had misplaced their reservations, and they ended up in a dark back room, intended, Peterson thought, for the kitchen help or the maintenance staff. Christine had brought along some lemon-flavored body oil as a surprise, and, although he would have liked to have been able to rise to the occasion, he found that all that he could manage was a lengthy foot and back massage, which seemed to satisfy her, instead.

 The next morning they toured the town. Christine had their itinerary efficiently scheduled. Breakfast of fresh-squeezed orange juice and pastry at a juice bar on the square. Morning at the market with its con men hawking Mayan handwork, its odors of shoe leather, fish, and lime. Lunch of cheese and bread and chili'd orange slices purchased from a street-side vendor. Afternoon at the local museum, and dinner of pollo pibil and Tekate at the hotel restaurant. That night Peterson threw up in the bougainvillea outside the hotel, and again in the shower as he tried to wash the day away with Rosa Venus soap.

 "I can't understand it," Christine said. "We've been so careful. No water, no salads, no ice cubes. You shouldn't be sick."

 It was not, Peterson thought, on her schedule.

He spent the next day between the shabby velvet sofa in the hotel lobby and the toilet in the dank bathroom, while Christine visited the cathedral and the market again on her own. She seemed happy here, he thought, as he slumped in the sofa, though her cheerfulness seemed more the forced cheer of duty than actual pleasure. She was doing this for him, and she was always happiest when she was helping someone else. She had wanted to join the Peace Corps when they were first married. She had done some volunteer work after her junior year in college at a settlement house in Chicago. Dropped off daily in a South side neighborhood and told to do "community organization," she wandered the streets and knocked on doors, feeling helpless until the riots prompted the organizers to send the volunteers home early. She had always felt that she had unfinished business, and she wanted Peterson to share that feeling.

"You're just selfish," she told him. "You don't care about anybody but yourself."

He wondered. He knew he didn't want to give up two years of his life to feel inept in Africa or Asia. He had a career he'd prepared for, and he wanted to get on with it. Besides, there wasn't anything necessarily more moral or important about digging latrines in Kenya than in teaching college, he argued. You were of most use to society where you performed best.

As he sat, frowning, wedged into the corner of the lumpy sofa in the Hotel Merida, staring out the front window at the street, his gut rumbling ominously, a young Mexican woman strolled past on the sidewalk, pausing in front of the window to check the reflection of her face. Peterson gazed aimlessly at her. She wasn't particularly attractive, he thought, her face painted in gaudy red lipstick, magenta rouge, and blue eye shadow, her nose broad and flat as if it had been punched in, her body squat and thick. Still, something about the sun on her long black hair, the cut of the leather miniskirt on her thighs, the thrust of her breasts above her black corset, the way her high-heeled boots forced her to walk, made him stir.

She glanced in at him, smiled and winked, rubbing her thumb and forefinger together quizzically. He imagined himself picking her up, taking her to his room, standing by the bed ... and then he could imagine no more. He smiled back, and shook his head.

He closed his eyes as a wave of nausea surged over him. Not counting his brief but passionate adolescent romance with Andrea in high school and the one unlikely encounter with Stefanie, Christine was the only woman he'd ever had sex with, and when he fantasized at all he could only seem to fantasize about her. In high school he had gotten the nickname "Peterless" after he refused to accompany some of his friends downtown to a St. Louis whorehouse. At least that's where they *said* they were going. For all their boasting, Peterson doubted that they'd really gone.

The young woman strolled back past the window, this time accompanied by a sleek mestizo in a white suit and a panama hat. They glided by like cats. Her embroidered blouse was unbuttoned almost to her waist; his arm snaked around her, and his hand cupped her breast. As they passed, Peterson thought she glanced his way for a moment, with a look almost of appeal, but then they were gone, leaving only the empty street.

Peterson shifted in his seat. With the exception of last night's body oil episode, he hadn't tried to make love to Christine for weeks. He blamed it on Jennifer, but he had never been very romantic with Christine, a fact that disturbed her.

"You just don't know how to give," she had told him.

Maybe she was right. Indeed, it did upset him the way she gave money to charity when their budget was already tight, or additional time to her volunteer work when he had expected her home for dinner.

"It's what's wrong with our whole culture," she was fond of saying. "Getting rather than giving determines your stature. The more you get, the bigger person you are."

His counter seemed weak, but he delivered it like a lecture. "If you give away everything, then you just join the ranks of the needy yourself."

He believed in being cautiously charitable with his time, his money, his energy. You had to hold *something* in reserve. The roof could rot, the car break down, your daughter be born defective. And when that happened he wanted to be prepared; he didn't want to have to ask for help.

He stared out into the street where some little Mexican children seemed to be playing a game with pesos. They'd throw them against the side of the stucco building and laugh, then retrieve them and throw again. The children were ragged and dirty—street urchins—but they were better off than Jennifer, he thought. Even the prostitute was better off than Jennifer. They, at least, had the present, if they had little future. Jennifer had nothing.

He'd worried about having a child in the first place. He didn't know how they would afford it, and he thought that it could change their lives in ways they couldn't predict. He remembered an episode of "Monty Python" he'd seen when they were first married. In one animated segment a fat baby was noisily sucking on a pacifier in a crib. Family members were sitting in the periphery of the frame. Suddenly a giant hand reached in from outside the frame and rested on the pacifier. "No!" shouted all the family members in unison. But the hand popped the pacifier from the baby's mouth, and the entire room and all its contents were sucked up screaming into the child. It had seemed hilarious at the time. Now it seemed prophetic.

Outside the hotel window, the young Mexican girl was back, once again alone. She was actually rather pretty, Peterson thought, under all the makeup and the ridiculous outfit. She glanced at him, her head cocked. He wondered if syphilis was a problem in Mexico; and, of course, there were other diseases. It would be just his luck. It was his policy, after all, to expect the worst. It was a way of always getting the best of any situation. If the worst happened, then at least he had predicted it. If the worst didn't happen, then his fears simply weren't confirmed. Either way, it made him feel on top of things. It was superstitious, he knew, but predicting disaster seemed a way of preventing it. It drove Christine crazy, however, and it hadn't worked with Jennifer. The worst had happened, and nothing he could do would change that.

The prostitute moved on. Maybe Christine was right—he needed to let go, live one day at a time, embrace life with its chances and risks. Nothing ever seemed to worry her for long, or keep her from doing exactly what she wanted to do. If she wanted to go skinny-dipping on their honeymoon in Minnesota despite the evening fishermen, if she wanted to garden topless in their plot behind the barn despite Goff and the neighbor kids with their binoculars, if she wanted to drive twice the speed limit past the police station, she did. He was the one who got poison ivy, bit by the dog, the ticket for double parking.

the sacred well

When she was driving too fast and following too close, and he reminded her that she should maintain one car-length from the car ahead for every ten miles per hour, she laughed that if he had his way she'd drive ten car-lengths behind the car she was in.

A scuffle in the street outside interrupted Peterson's revery. The tall mestizo in the panama hat had grabbed the prostitute by the hair and was dragging her across the street. She was screaming something in Spanish and struggling to free herself. She glanced wildly toward the hotel as the man slapped her and she slumped against him whimpering. Peterson got to his feet, paused as a surge of nausea unsteadied him. He was sick, he rationalized, as he stumbled toward the bathroom. And besides, it wasn't any of his business.

That night his dreams were punctuated by screaming babies, airstrips, whores in doorways, nausea, and Christine nuzzling up to him happy in the damp sheets.

The next morning, feeling somewhat better, Peterson agreed to accompany Christine to the Mayan ruins at Chichen Itza. They hired a driver through the hotel tourist service, got in the back seat of his beat-up Volkswagen, and drove out the narrow highway to the ruins. Now Christine was pumping Carlos for information.

"Sisal," he said. "The workers pick sisal. Ten, twelve hours a day. It makes good rope, sisal. You know it?"

Christine said she didn't.

"We stop at a sisal factory," he said. "You will see how it is made. The workers pick the sisal and twist its fibers into rope. You see sisal baskets maybe in America. We send many baskets to America. Workers get maybe two dollars a day, maybe more. You would like to pick sisal maybe?" He pointed out the window at the grass and mud huts. "Mayan. They live like this for hundreds of years, before the Spanish bring Christianity and disease. I am mestizo, but I feel Mayan. For many years we are not proud to be Mayan. We want to be like gringos. Now we are proud to be Mayan."

Christine was jotting everything down in her little book. "Oh, and those trees. What are they called?" She pointed at some small clumps of trees, growing almost like shrubs at the edge of the jungle.

"Oh, those are gumbo-limbo. Sometimes called tourist trees because they are red and peeling." He smiled broadly into the back seat.

Christine made a notation.

"Many jaguars on this road. You cannot walk on this road without a rifle." He pointed to a man in the distance. "Many jaguars. This is a dangerous jungle. Jaguars, snakes. We patrol roads to keep jaguars away. We also keep jungle away. We cut it back and cut it back. In six months there would be no road. The jungle would take it. It is easy to get lost in the jungle here."

When they arrived at the ruins, Peterson was disappointed. It may once have been jungle, but now it was more like a park. The lawns were neatly seeded and mowed. There was an expensive hotel that looked out over the pyramids, and the large parking lot was full of tour buses.

"You go with one of the tours," Carlos said. "That way you get good talk on the ruins. I come back later and pick you up." He tipped his straw hat and was gone.

"What now?" Peterson asked.

the sacred well

"We join a tour," Christine said.

They slipped into the back of a group of twenty or so American tourists, and moved from site to site, Peterson snapping pictures of the ball court where losers were decapitated; the Chac Mools with their hollowed-out vessels for holding human hearts; the statues of Quetzalcoatl, the feathered serpent, with his demands for flesh and blood; the cenote, the sacred well, with its sacrificial virgins. Violence and sacrifice, Peterson thought. Violence and sacrifice. That was what made the whole world work. The helpless and crippled and weak consigned to the ball court, the Chac Mool, the cenote, the sisal field, the street, for the well-being of the powerful other. Religion, myth, ritual, wealth—how they rendered rage and pain sacred.

"Peterson!" Christine's voice brought him back. "What are you doing?" In his revery Peterson had been removing the used film from the camera, preparing to insert another roll. He had forgotten to rewind the finished roll, and opening the camera he had exposed the last few pictures. He quickly closed the camera, rewound the film, and replaced it.

"I'm sick to death of it," she was saying. "I'm not strong enough for both of us. I'm tired of your silence and depression. I'm tired of your endless self-pity. You're dragging me down, you're trying to pull me in after you. I thought this trip would be good for us, would bring us back together. You've got to face up to it. I can't do it for you. You've got to take some responsibility. Jennifer's not the problem, Peterson. *You* are."

Peterson stared stupidly at her for a moment. She stared back at him.

"I'm sorry," Peterson said. It was all he could manage.

He looked at the hard blue sky, and then at the dense jungle. He didn't look at Christine. "I'm going back to retake some pictures," he said.

He turned from the group slowly and began jogging back past the statue of Quetzalcoatl and the long frieze of skulls, through the small opening in the jungle, and down the path to the cenote. She was right, of course, but things seemed to be out of his hands. He hadn't her competence and efficiency. He hadn't her generosity of spirit. He hadn't her resilience and control. He didn't know what he could do.

He found himself standing on the edge of the cenote, the sacred well. It was utterly silent. The wind had died in the trees, and the tourists had all disappeared. He thought about Jennifer, her microcephalia. He remembered a series of Li'l Abner comics he had read when he was in grade school. Some villain had come up with a shrinking potion and shrunk Li'l Abner's head to the size of a pea. It didn't seem to have affected Li'l Abner's intelligence at all, but it had affected his good looks. The oversized, muscled body with its pea-sized head wasn't so much funny as it was uncomfortably compelling, and Peterson had avidly bought the Sunday paper with his own allowance each Saturday night from the paperboy who pulled his wagon around the neighborhood, rather than waiting for the regular delivery Sunday morning. Now, when he thought about Jennifer as an adult, he pictured her as Li'l Abner. He couldn't remember how Li'l Abner had gotten his head back to normal size.

He looked out over the cenote. It was not particularly impressive—just a round hole in the earth about fifty feet in diameter, ringed by smooth boulders and scrub vegetation. He edged carefully up to the rim to try to see down into it, but was unable to see anything except the gray stone on the far side falling into shadow. They had recovered valuable artifacts from this well, the guide had said—rings, bracelets, precious stones, pottery, bones. It appeared now that not only virgins were tossed in to appease the gods, but young boys and old men as well. What exactly the purposes of the rites were, no one knew. Perhaps to improve the weather or the crops, defeat the enemy, cure the illnesses of the priests, or just to get rid of strangers and cripples.

Perched on the edge, Peterson listened to the silence. It was heavy and thick, palpable as humidity. He stared at the jungle with its poisonous snakes and jaguars, and thought of the sisal fields beyond, and the streets of Merida, and the Caribbean, and Miami, and Chicago. The gumbo-limbo trees, red and peeling, crowded toward him. The round circle of the well, nondescript as it was, had a curious attraction. Peterson slipped his hand into his pocket as he stared at the smooth stone, withdrew a silver coin and flipped it in. It vanished soundlessly into the abyss. He strained to hear it land, but could not.

The silence surrounded him like cloth, like a second skin. He took his camera off his shoulder and held it to the sun. He had bought this camera, an expensive 35 mm Nikon, years ago when he was in graduate school and unable to afford the monthly rent, much less a camera. It had wiped his small savings account clean, but he had wanted it. Gleaming in the sun now, it seemed somehow cold and alien. He gazed at it a moment, and then, taking a deep breath and leaning back, he threw it in. It disappeared in silence.

He thought he could hear voices in the distance, perhaps another tour group approaching, but he didn't care. He felt somehow strong and pure. He removed his shoes and socks, his shirt and pants, and tossed them over the edge. They lifted in the windless air, twisting like birds or feathered serpents, hovering a moment in slow motion before sinking into oblivion. He removed his underpants, and, wadding them into a skull-sized bundle, threw them in.

The voices sounded louder now, a muffled concatenation, a din. It was not the direction tourists should be coming from. He stood naked in the sun feeling strangely light and sexual. He looked at the jungle. The jungle looked at him.

*n*o
answer

If only she hadn't been so pink and steamy. I think that was it, the pink and the steam, the glow of her nude body in the tub as she lay gazing somewhere beyond me, the way women who should wear glasses, but don't, look through you dreamily. Perhaps it was the pink and the steam and the heat in the white-tiled bathroom, our five-year-old daughter, Jennifer, sitting on the edge of the closed toilet, watching us watch each other, saying, "Mommy's naked, Daddy. Why are you staring?"

The phone in the bedroom was ringing. It was Andrea. She was calling from the cabin she'd rented in the Adirondacks, to see if I could get free. After twenty-five years she'd written me from Paris to say she loved me after all, and she'd be in the States this weekend. For twenty-five years I'd dreamed of her, and how the full moon had shown through the open back window of my father's old Ford on her small breasts. And now she was back, wanting me.

"The phone's ringing," my daughter said.

"Aren't you going to answer it?" my wife smiled dreamily.

"Yes," I said, mesmerized by the steamy scene, the glow of her blurred nudity.

"Wash my back," she pouted.

The phone rang on through the pink and the steam and the old Ford and the moon.

"Now beat it, you big buffoon," she laughed, "so I can get out of the tub."

"Beat it," my daughter crooned.

I stood in the drafty hallway, musing. What was I doing? The phone rang on, desire still fast in its cradle.

When Christine stepped out in the hall fully clothed, her mouth in its thin set line, her languor and loveliness gone, our daughter hard behind her, the phone stopped ringing. And the phone rang on.

logjam

It wasn't his fault. When they pulled into the campground, conditions were as bad as they could possibly be. The weather report called for high winds and hail. Four inches of rain had fallen in thirty minutes just sixty miles to the west of them, and the sky was an ominous shade of greenish-black. Mosquitoes hung like gauze in the heavy air. When he got out of the car to check the campsite, they shrouded him, and he danced like a marionette to their music. Yes, he thought, with his red hair and freckles and his stupid forced grin, he felt exactly like Howdy Doody dancing for the Peanut Gallery and selling Wonder Bread. Their ten-year-old daughter, Phoebe, was doing her best to be Flub-a-Dub or Clarabelle, and his wife, Christine, glaring from the car, was grim as Phineas T. Bluster.

It dated him, he thought. No one under the age of forty (except Phoebe and Jennifer, perhaps, who had heard his stories of the fifties numerous times, told in the hyperbolic style he adopted to amuse them) would have made the comparison.

"It looks good," he shouted through the drone of mosquitoes and the Nova's closed windows.

Phoebe forced a smile, and Christine only glared.

It was the last day of their great Eastern car trip—something Christine had wanted to do for years. Jennifer, twelve and unwilling to leave the goats and chickens she raised on their recreational farm, had stayed home with Peterson's approval and to Christine's consternation. Christine's mother agreed to stay with her. Peterson, Christine, and Phoebe had driven 3,500 miles from Wisconsin to Cape Cod and then to Bar Harbor and Montreal, and were now in a Provincial Park in Canada. The park was called "The Chutes" because of the old wooden chutes that were designed to get logs past the small waterfall and through the rapids without jamming. The logging had denuded the countryside, and the whole area, all scrub pine and fir, even fifty years later seemed stunted or blighted.

"Get back in the car," Christine mouthed through the window.

They had followed Christine's plans exactly. In Cape Cod they stayed in Wellfleet, going to Provincetown only once to let Phoebe shop for an hour and take a whale-watching cruise. They had visited the beach once for two hours, slathered with the #45 sunblock Christine had brought, and spent the rest of the time hiking and bicycling in the National Seashore. Christine despised idleness. A vacation for her meant driving fourteen hours one day to get somewhere so you could hike fourteen hours the next.

They spent a day on an island off Bar Harbor, owned by one of Christine's uncles, hiking its seven-mile circumference through pine woods and over steep cliffs in the cold fog, and then a day driving to Quebec for a four-hour tour of the Old City before pushing to Toronto and beyond.

He would have preferred to sit on the beach or leisurely beachcomb, or spend a day poking around the Provincetown or Bar Harbor shops. But this was Christine's trip, and he was determined to be agreeable. He was, he admitted, even glad for her enthusiasms. If she hadn't pushed them over the years to go backpacking in the Rockies, rafting on the Colorado, tramping through the jungles of the Yucatan, and now driving through New England and Canada, they would never have left Wisconsin at all. He knew that it was good for them, and he was trying to be accommodating. If she wanted to camp, they'd camp, despite the abysmal conditions.

"Where's the mosquito repellent?" he asked from the front passenger's seat, as pleasantly as possible.

She fumbled around in the glove compartment, and then in her purse.

"I don't know what happened to it," she announced. "Maybe we don't have any. I can't think of everything."

He knew she knew he didn't want to camp, and it was making her surly. The more agreeable he was, the more she was sure of his insincerity. It had become a code between them. Whenever they were really angry or irritated, they would kill each other with kindness. It made it increasingly difficult *really* to be nice, when niceness itself was a weapon.

"Look," she said sweetly. "We don't have to camp if you don't want to."

"I want to," he assured her.
"Really, we could just stay in a motel."
"We do want to camp," Phoebe gamely piped up.
He marveled at how easy lying was for her. She could tell her mother anything she wanted to hear and make her believe it. Even he believed it this time, for a moment. It was enough to determine his resolve.
"Why don't you go into town," he offered, "and get some mosquito repellent. We'll set up the tent."
Thunder was rumbling all around them and the sky was blackening fast, but there wasn't a breath of wind. The mosquitoes whined like a bad connection.
"We'll use our machetes on them," he joked, sliding out of the car and motioning Phoebe to follow.
He and Phoebe set busily about the tent, while Christine slammed the Nova into gear, spun the tires, and drove off, faster than the narrow sandy park road quite allowed.
"I hate it when you guys do that," Phoebe frowned.
He was tempted to draw her out with a "Do what?" or a "So do I," but the mosquitoes whined insistently, and he knew he shouldn't martial his daughter's support in a conflict with her mother.
"Better stake it down good," he said. "The storm is coming." He separated the ridge poles from the side poles and began popping them into place.
How had they managed to live together for nearly twenty years, he wondered? When they were first married, it was different. Christine was sweet and reasonable, innocent and shy. She hadn't really dated anyone other than him and Frank, and, with her Scotch Presbyterian upbringing, had led a sheltered life. She seemed happy to

keep house, cook, see her friends, and do her volunteer work. But soon she began to seem dissatisfied. Although she rarely complained directly about anything, she began to grow hard and testy. She debated him on insignificant issues just, he thought, out of irritability. He would mention some trivial problem at work, the kind of thing he didn't really want any more response to than a smile or a nod, and she'd find some way to argue an opposite side.

"The Dean's pushing us to publish again," he'd say. "What does he want from us, anyway?"

"Well, he probably has a good reason for it," she'd say.

"Yeah, to make him look good."

"It's probably good for the whole college. He's probably just more ambitious than some of the faculty."

"You mean me."

"I'm not saying you should be more ambitious."

"What *are* you saying?"

"Oh, I'm just trying to understand why you're upset," she'd smile.

"I'm not all that upset."

"You seem pretty upset."

"I'm just telling you what happened today. I'm just letting off a little steam."

"Sounds like more than that to me."

"I don't want to talk about it," he'd say, and walk away.

"Why are you walking away from me? I thought we were having a conversation," she'd call, steely, after him.

"I don't want to argue."

"It's not an argument, it's a conversation. You think any time I don't agree with you, it's an argument. You want me to pretend to agree? You don't want my honest feelings?"

After a two-hour debate she'd seem rejuvenated, energized, and he'd be exhausted, depleted. She loved these discussions, said they were important to a healthy relationship. He hated them and thought they were symptoms of a disease. Her theory was that it was best to get it all out; confrontation therapy appealed to her. His theory was that it was better to keep it all in; to articulate a problem, where the merest shadow of one existed, was to give that shadow palpable shape and energy.

And so they argued. They argued about dependency. She insisted it was bad. The very word "dependency," she said, suggested weakness, addiction, and sickness, while "independence" suggested strength and self-reliance.

"Need is weakness," she'd say. "I don't want to be needy."

"But love is based on need," he'd counter. "If we don't need each other and depend on each other, why, what then?"

"What you mean," she'd reply, "is that you want everything your way. If we women are strong," she'd say, echoing her assertiveness training group, "you men think it weakens you."

So the power shifted from his benevolent monarchy to her reign of terror, her strong-arm dictatorship. She felt, it seemed, that she always had to be on her guard, lest he should wrest that power back. But he just gave it up to her. No contest. She decided what was best for Jennifer and Phoebe; she handled the money; she organized their social engagements and planned her elaborate trips.

She wanted to ensure that their daughters had the opportunities she felt she had never had. "I want the girls to know that they can be anything they want to be, do anything they want to do," she would say. By which she meant, he pointed out, anything that Christine approved of, anything politically correct and powerful. Jennifer and Phoebe could be doctors or lawyers or engineers. They couldn't be housewives, or maids, or bag ladies. And when Jennifer expressed a desire to do just that, or nothing, with her life, expressing her own independence, it drove Christine crazy. When he defended Jennifer's lack of appropriate "ambition," Christine merely countered, "You wouldn't say that if she were a boy." He wondered.

Inside the tent, dispatching the mosquitoes that had followed them, they rolled out the sleeping bags and arranged the packs.

"Why do you?" Phoebe asked.

"What?" he said.

"Do that."

She had raised such issues with disturbing frequency, and it placed him in a difficult position. If he supported Christine against his own judgment, he was being unfair to Phoebe. If he sympathized with Phoebe, following his natural inclinations, he was betraying Christine. He wanted Phoebe to know he respected and valued her feelings, even shared them, but he didn't want to martial her as an ally.

"We all get a little impatient sometimes," he replied. "I guess I do too."

From inside the tent they heard the sound of tires spinning on the sandy park road, a screech of brakes, and a crash of underbrush. Then there was the sound of a car backing up. It whined through the heavy air like a giant mosquito. Then silence, a door slamming, and footsteps.

Christine had been hurrying back with the mosquito

repellent, he conjectured, she had run off the road, and it was his fault.

She slipped into the tent and zipped up the mosquito netting.

"Look," she said brightly, her face in a tight smile, her voice lilting. "Let's not camp."

He knew how mad she was by how extremely pleasant she was being.

"Neither of you really wants to camp," she continued, "and I'd be just as happy to go to a motel. I passed several nice ones in town with vacancies. It's going to rain and there are mosquitoes. Besides, we should have the headlight repaired."

The headlight? There was something ridiculously funny in all of this, he thought. He wondered if he just started laughing she would see the humor in it and they'd all start laughing, dismissing all the tension and hostility as their laughter rang out into the night over the drone of the boring mosquitoes and the impotent roar of the storm. He pictured the three of them for a moment, alone on this earth in their small warm place, their laughter sailing out into the universe.

Outside the wind whipped through the trees and the rain began in earnest. No. He wasn't about to let her outcharm him.

"Well," he smiled. "We've got the tent all set up and we all want to camp." Small hail began pelleting the tent like popcorn, the taut nylon fabric snapping merrily. "The rain will probably pass, and the mosquitoes aren't that bad."

"Oh, but the weather report," Christine said. "And look at all those bites on poor Phoebe."

Phoebe was a large red welt in the corner of the tent, a flurry of itch.

"Phoebe's happy to stay here," he smiled.

"Phoebe would rather go to a motel," she smiled back.

"Phoebe ..."

"Phoebe ..."

Phoebe, propped in her dark corner, closed her eyes and squinched her face into a grotesque stiff grin. "Hey, kids!" she screamed, her voice all crackle and static, "What time is it?"

Outside, the storm howled and whistled. Inside, their smiles sluiced faster and faster through the dark, like logs slipping unimpeded down an ancient long chute.

jackknife

He thought she didn't love him anymore. Relations between them had been strained, to say the least. As they sat there at the picnic table at their farmhouse in Prairie County, Wisconsin, the weedy box elders and dead or dying elms stretching off in the gully like a broken promise, a mockingbird twirping merrily on a fence post, he wondered.

Their ten-year-old daughter, Phoebe, oblivious to the tension in the air, was twirping merrily, too, something about lost jackknives and miraculous recoveries. "Isn't that amazing?" she twittered, flapping her small arms and levitating a good three feet above the table.

"Slow down," he said, though he knew she was just frantically happy they were all back together. He gazed across the gully at the hillside glistening with the first rain in weeks, the oak trees dim and shimmering under the broken clouds. "Listen," he said. "Here's a story about a jackknife—a true story. When I was a kid, about your age, Phoebe, my father took me fishing in Minnesota. The first day out I accidentally dropped his favorite jackknife over the side of the boat. We were fishing the deep water for Northerns, and, though he solemnly proposed lowering me down on a line to retrieve it, it was lost. Two days later, I caught the biggest Northern I'd ever seen—must have been ten pounds. When my father cut it open ..."

"Oh, come on," his wife began, but he talked over her.

"When he cut that Northern open in the fish house late that night—this is a *true* story—the pearl-handled jackknife wasn't there! No. That jackknife was lost. We never found it."

There was a moment of silence. The sun had set behind the black clouds in the hollow, and the spring peepers had begun their tremulous warbling in old man Goff's horse pond. And then his wife was laughing, and his daughters too, their voices like bright goldfinches high on the wires, or tiny bells swelling in the distance, ringing from runnel to rivulet, the whole valley lit like a crystal glass of milk, spring peepers coupling in the lush romantic dusk.

animal rights

They were sitting in the Chicago airport, waiting for their flight to Sarasota, and the U.S. government was torturing cats. The cats were consigned to dark cramped cages, not big enough to stand up in, where they starved and went crazy. Their luminous eyes were round and insane, their screams like the screams of a flayed baby.

Every day when the government scientists arrived for work they would take a cat from its cage, strap its frail matted body into a special harness, clamp its head in a vise, and, placing a military assault rifle behind its ear, shoot it.

The government was studying the effects of head wounds on foot soldiers and using cats as subjects. Cats, the military spokesman explained, were a good deal like foot soldiers. Unsurprisingly, the cats' heads were blown off, and the resultant wounds caused the cats to become disoriented and to have difficulty breathing or functioning fully as cats. The research suggested that a similar thing would happen, and indeed many times *had* happened, to soldiers who were wounded similarly at the front.

"Isn't that disgusting, Mother?" said Jennifer, who had been summarizing the article from her *Alliance for Animals* magazine. "Somewhere in this city they are torturing cats, and we're sitting in the airport doing nothing!"

Christine nodded and closed her eyes. Somewhere behind the low plaint of her daughter's voice, in the hum and buzz of the crowd, she could almost hear the growl of the starved subjects, feel their unbearable pain. The overpriced hot dog in her hand, smothered with mustard and pickle relish, leaking its meaty juices onto her napkin, had begun to lose some of its savor. Why did Jennifer have to spoil everything? she thought. Why couldn't she just enjoy a trip with her mother to Florida without dragging along her baggage of obsessions?

"Listen to this," Jennifer read from her magazine. "In a lifetime, the average meat-eater will consume eight cattle, thirty-six sheep, thirty-six pigs, five-hundred-fifty chickens, and one-half ton of fish."

Christine stopped chewing, the flesh moist and salty on her tongue.

"How's your dead pig, Mother?" Jennifer said.

How Jennifer had changed, Christine thought. So aggressive, and accusatory, and angry now. As a child, Jennifer had been shy—afraid, it seemed, of everything. Perhaps it was a result of her misdiagnosis as a microcephalic, and the strain it had put on Christine and Peterson. When Jennifer finally began growing normally, Christine thought, the psychological damage had probably already been done. Jennifer was afraid of the bathroom faucet, which tended to stick and then come on with a rush; she was afraid to put the needle down on her record player for fear of its scratch and blare. "Just be the boss of it," Christine told her. "Just you be the boss of it," she said. But nothing Christine said seemed to matter.

Once, when they arrived home from Jennifer's grade school in the rain, Jennifer wouldn't leave the car. She was afraid she might step on worms that had surfaced on the sidewalk. "Carry me!" she pleaded. Christine, thinking Jennifer needed to face her fears and overcome them (she *was* eight years old, after all), said simply, "Come in when you're ready, dear," and walked into the house, leaving the door ajar on Jennifer's hysterical tears. After an hour in the car, evening coming on with its own trepidations, Jennifer finally made a run for the house and threw herself into her mother's arms. "I know I shouldn't be scared," she cried. "But I am!"

It was hard for Christine to know what to do. She didn't want to coddle her daughter, and yet she didn't want to be too hard on her either. She didn't want to do everything herself for Jennifer, but then Jennifer seemed so helpless.

She couldn't count on much from Peterson, who was struggling to get tenure at the college and had once told her he hadn't wanted a child in the first place. Peterson had nearly had a nervous breakdown himself over Jennifer's inexplicable medical problems, and had never, since then, wanted to press Jennifer to do anything. Perhaps if he had expected more from her, been a little tougher on her. But it just wasn't in his nature.

Jennifer flipped the page in her magazine, humming loudly one of her favorite Pete and Lou Berryman songs: "Gonna have a big dead bird for dinnerrrr ... on Christma-as day."

A large woman in a fur coat, her face sculpted in makeup, standing in line at the check-in, glanced at them and smiled at Christine sympathetically.

Jennifer smiled back at the woman. "How's your dead mink?" she said under her breath.

"Jennifer," Christine cautioned.

Jennifer's obsessions had once been just a frustration, a concern, an annoyance; now they were an embarrassment, Christine thought. Last Thanksgiving, Christine had had her mother and father and her next door neighbor Susan, a divorced family therapist, for dinner. When Christine asked Jennifer to help serve, Jennifer complied, carrying the dishes to the table, singing loudly that song: "Gonna have a big dead bird for dinnerrrr ..." Phoebe thought it was hysterically funny. Everyone else laughed nervously, and Peterson only smiled as Christine glared at him.

Susan had brought a Jell-O salad, and about halfway through the meal Jennifer set down her fork and interrupted the conversation. "Wait a minute," she said. "What's gelatin made from?"

The table was silent for a moment, and then Christine's father, Douglas, said authoritatively, "Cow's hooves."

Jennifer put her hand to her mouth, and gagged. "Oh, my God!" she screamed, and fled to the bathroom where the sounds of her retching filled the air.

"What was that all about?" Douglas asked.

Christine explained, and they went on with the dinner, everyone smiling understandingly.

As it turned out, Jennifer's display was not the most memorable embarrassment of the afternoon. Shortly after Jennifer fled, Susan commented on an ad she'd seen for turkey dinner at a local restaurant.

"I can't imagine anyone going *out* for Thanksgiving dinner!" she said.

"Oh, it's the biggest day of the year for restaurants. Bigger than Christmas," Douglas said.

"Don't you think most people stay home, or go to friends' or family's houses for Thanksgiving?" Christine's mother, Ruth, said.

"No," Douglas said louder. "Thanksgiving is bigger even than Christmas for restaurants." Douglas was animated now, and insistent.

"Well, I'm glad I'm *here*," said Susan. "It's a great dinner, Christine."

"Well, I could just call up a restaurant," Douglas said. "You name it. Name any restaurant and we'll call them and ask them if it's their biggest day. I think you'll find I'm right!"

"That's not necessary," Ruth said. "We believe you."

"Ovens of Brittany? Let's just call Ovens of Brittany," Douglas said, rising unsteadily from the table. He went to the phone in the living room, and dialed. "Yes, I'll hold," he said. "See?" he called back into the dining room. "They're busy!"

Christine glanced at her mother. Ruth shrugged and said nothing.

Douglas cleared his throat loudly to keep their attention, and then, "How busy are you today?" he all but shouted. "I mean, I'm just checking, is this your busiest day of the year? No, I don't want to make a reservation.

Can you just tell me how busy you are? Thank you." He put down the phone and returned to the dining room. "Busiest day of the year!" he said. "I knew it."

"Somewhere they are torturing cats," Jennifer said again. "I hate airports. Everybody walking around so smug and complacent. Like robots—no idea what's going on out there. Wasn't it around here somewhere, under the airport, that they made the atom bomb? The one that murdered the Japanese?"

"That was under the stadium," Christine said.

"The world is insane," Jennifer said.

Murdered the Japanese, Christine thought. Well, that was one way to put it, she supposed. Her father, who had lost a leg in the war, had looked at it similarly.

"They didn't have to drop it," he argued. "Look at me. We didn't need more of this sort of thing."

Once, in one of his bitter moods, he had told Christine how a buddy of his had killed a "Jap" and cut his heart out and put it in a jar as a souvenir. "He brought it to the hospital to show me, and we laughed. We laughed. 'Good for you,' I told him. War does things to a man," he said. Christine's father carried a suitcase, a portable bar, with him everywhere. "My anesthesia," he said. Her father had managed to become a successful physician in town despite his disability, but his anger burned on. How had her mother endured it—her father's bitterness and rage and self-flagellation? Ruth had been a saint. No matter how torn up she must have been inside, she always seemed placid, composed. Christine idolized her. When Christine's friends complained about their mothers,

Christine just sat back, silent. Her mother was perfect; she had no complaints.

Though now Christine saw that her mother had repressed a great deal—and even harbored some hostilities toward Christine. Shortly after Jennifer's birth, Ruth came to visit, to help take care of the house. Peterson was incapacitated by panic. In one of their long conversations one evening, Christine asked her mother if in any way Christine had been a disappointment to her. Was there anything she wished Christine had done differently? Ruth said no, but then on reflection she said, "I wish you had stayed in the church."

Christine was silent.

"Religion is what gives us strength," Ruth said.

"Your strength comes from yourself," Christine said.

"Are you …" Ruth hesitated, "going to have Jennifer baptized?"

The thought hadn't occurred to Christine. "I don't know, Mother," she said.

After that, she did think about it—she worried to Peterson that they weren't even giving Jennifer the chance to reject religion as they had. But she didn't do anything further about it. Occasionally she still thought about it, and, though her mother never brought it up again, it remained a small wedge between them. What other grievances was her mother keeping to herself? Christine vowed always to be honest with Jennifer—to articulate her anger and disappointment. And Jennifer had given her ample opportunity.

Christine stared out the plane window at the flying dog. It was strapped to a table, and a dozen electrodes proceeded from its face and sexual organs. They were studying the effects of immobilization on sexual activity. The theory was that immobilization would hamper it. Indeed, the dog did not seem to be very aroused.

"How can anyone permit this stuff?" Jennifer said. "How can anyone condone such atrocities?"

Christine's arguments about the need for animal research—how it had resulted in cures for polio, diabetes, heart disease—paled in the face of Jennifer's graphic testimonies. Jennifer wasn't impressed with the fact that even the mother of Jane Goodall, one of her heroes, had a pig valve in her heart.

"What if you were dying?" Christine asked.

"I would rather die myself than kill an animal so I could live," Jennifer retorted.

"What if *I* were dying?" Christine twisted the knife.

"Why are we so egotistical that we think we have the right to kill another species?" Jennifer said. "It's what I hate about Christianity." She infused the word "Christianity" with utter contempt. "Christianity says God made the animals for us, to torture and master and eat. It's horrible."

Out the window of the plane a dozen flying mice, deprived of arms and legs, raced alongside them, strangely translucent and unencumbered.

The stewardess clattered by with her cart of chicken kiev, a small football of meat on a plastic plate, flanked by an anemic crowd of broccoli and carrots. Jennifer shuddered in disgust.

"I think we'll pass," Christine said.

The stewardess smiled sweetly and trundled on.

Christine had tried vegetarianism herself years ago, she remembered, back when she and Peterson were first married. Peterson had just gotten his teaching job, and Christine was working part-time. It was fun at first, taking turns with the *Moosewood Cookbook*, but gradually Peterson began hazarding the mystery meat in the college cafeteria, and Christine sneaked off to McDonald's on her lunch hour, and eventually they abandoned the experiment, assuring themselves that they would eat *less* meat, anyway.

They were over Nashville now, encountering some turbulence. In the seasonless uniformity of the plane, it was easy to forget the sub-zero February wasteland they had left in Wisconsin, with its frozen pipes, its treacherous iced-over streets, the lakes stretched out cold and unforgiving, the sky blank as a bad idea, everyone insulated in down and wool. The turbulence increased. The cabin bells rang, and the FASTEN SEAT BELT sign flashed on. "Sorry for the inconvenience," the pilot's casual and sonorous voice lilted through the speakers. "I hope this doesn't spoil your dinner."

Christine wondered if pilots were hired, in part, for their voices, their ability to project calm and confidence in any situation. "We've lost both engines, and the wings are on fire, ladies and gentlemen. Sorry for the inconvenience." "World War III has broken out, the planet is gone, and there's no place to land. I hope this doesn't spoil your dinner."

"Listen to this," Jennifer was saying as the plane bumped and lurched like an aging carnival ride. "Pain, frustration, stress, fear, abuse, neglect, and deprivation are inherent in the predominant systems of rearing animals on today's factory farms. The young are removed before they are weaned, the lights are kept on constantly or not at all. Their horns, beaks, tails, and other 'unessential' body parts are mutilated or removed. They are kicked, prodded, electro-shocked, drugged, and finally transported to their deaths." Her voice rose in pitch and volume. The passenger next to her shifted in his seat, and leaned away into the aisle, holding his spreadsheet. She would not make a good pilot, Christine thought.

Jennifer had never responded well to stress. When a boy at high school, horsing around, had caught one of her tight waist-length braids in the zipper of his leather jacket, and ripped the braid out, leaving a bald spot the size of a half dollar, and then, not realizing what had happened, had laughed as his girlfriend picked up the braid and twirled it around, saying "Look everybody, fake hair!" Jennifer had shrieked and shrieked in agony. "You're a loony," the boy said.

At home that afternoon Jennifer wept uncontrollably. "My hair!" she cried. "My hair is the only thing I've got and now it's gone forever." That night Christine heard her banging her head against the wall by her bed, moaning low.

The bald spot had not filled in, and there was some concern that the trauma would cause additional hair loss. But by changing her part, and combing the hair out across it, Jennifer managed to cover it up. She stopped seeing her high school friends, and she became more obsessed with animal rights and vegetarianism.

Every Tuesday and Thursday Lydia would stop at the house in her old Toyota pickup to take Jennifer to the meetings. Lydia was a plain, undistinguished mouse of a woman, who seemed to Christine predominantly grim and taciturn. She was short and dumpy, her thin hair spiked up, her demeanor that of every wallflower Christine had dismissed in college. She was probably in her twenties, but could easily have been forty. So unlike Jennifer, beautiful Jennifer, Christine thought, who, if only she fixed herself up, could have been a model.

The meetings were held in the red-light district of town, on the south side of the square where rents were low, and Christine worried that Jennifer would be raped or molested. "Be careful," she said every time Jennifer left, and she stayed up until her daughter was safely home, which was sometimes well after midnight.

Recently the Alliance had demonstrated against the primate center at the zoo that supplied monkeys for the University's research. When a lab was broken into and trashed (by animal rights activists, the University said; by graduate research assistants trying to give the activists a bad name, said the Alliance), Jennifer was arrested and remanded to Christine's custody.

Jennifer seemed shaken by the experience, and Christine hoped that it would change her attitude. But the arrest seemed merely to reinforce her dedication to the cause. Jennifer was not only a vegetarian now, but a vegan, eating only those vegetables and fruits that fell naturally from the plant or tree. Anything that required taking the whole plant—radishes, carrots, peanuts, onions—she would not eat. She spoke admiringly of those Hindus and Tibetan monks who would sweep the path before them as they walked, so as not to risk stepping on even the slightest creature. When Christine asked, somewhat sarcastically, one night, if Jennifer's concern extended to microbes, bacteria, and viruses, Jennifer began to refuse all medications, or items with animal by-products or proteins. She lost weight. Her hair, once full and rich, in masses to her waist, grew limp and thin. Anger protruded from her like bristles.

Christine wondered if she should take her to a psychiatrist. "When I was your age," she told Jennifer, "I was going out every weekend with my friends, having fun. All you do is sit in your room and read. And speaking of your room, it's a pigsty."

"Pigs are among the cleanest of animals," Jennifer said.

Christine asked her friend Susan about it.

"Don't worry," Susan assured her. "My son spent two years sitting in his bed picking his toes. It's normal," she said.

When Christine finally confronted Jennifer directly, Jennifer blurted out, "You don't want me around here, you just want your *dreams* for me."

"Let's take a trip together," Christine said. "It will do us both good."

The seatbelt sign went off as the plane settled back into its smooth, reassuring hum.

"Listen to this," Jennifer said, tapping her magazine.

And Christine listened.

When the plane landed in Sarasota, the hatches opened to a blast of heavy humid air. Ruth was waiting at the gate with Douglas, arm in arm like young lovers, and all together they left the terminal for the key with its streetside bougainvillea, its egrets and anhingas roosting in the palm trees.

"It's wonderful," Jennifer said, lighting up in the sun. Her face seemed fuller, and her hair shone golden. "Look at the birds! And the trees!"

The warm air surrounded them like a hot springs, a massage. Douglas laughed, the white hairs on his barrel chest sticking out of his unbuttoned shirt. "Wait till you see the condo and the beach, sweetheart."

They spent the afternoon in the sand, white as the snow they had left behind, cool in the February sun, watching the porpoises leap and antic, the pelicans and cormorants loop and dive.

That night at dinner, between bites of meatless lasagna, Douglas turned to Jennifer. "I don't know what you've got against meat," he said. "Things die and they just go to waste. They just decay. Somebody might as well get some good out of it. Hell, animals eat each other, you know. It's just nature's way. Farm animals, by and large, have better lives than animals in the wild. It's in the farmers' best interests to keep their animals happy—they produce more milk and meat."

"That's not the point," Jennifer began.

"I thought that's what you wanted," Douglas interrupted, talking louder. "Happy animals! Believe me, they're better off on the farms. Where do you want to put all the cows, anyway. Out on the beach?"

"I just think it's wrong to kill creatures, to imprison them."

"Imprison them!" Douglas exploded. "They're not people!"

"I was just reading," Ruth said, changing the subject, "how the Japanese were interred during World War II—innocent American citizens—men, women, and children, treated like enemies."

"You don't know anything about it," Douglas shot back. "You don't know the first thing. I was in Intelligence. We knew things nobody else knew. The Japanese were a threat to national security. It was one of their plans—insurrection from within. If we hadn't stopped them ... It just makes me sick when people talk about what they don't know anything about."

Ruth looked at her plate. Jennifer stabbed at her lasagna.

"You just better be glad we did what we did, what we had to do," Douglas continued.

"You must be right," Christine said. "You're talking louder than the rest of us, so you must be right."

"Christine," Ruth intervened.

Douglas glared at Christine. Then, grinning, he said, "Well, now, anybody for fishing tomorrow?"

That night the sunset bled over the water, a giant killing floor, all sparkle and dazzle and rivulets of bright color. Jennifer and Christine walked along the beach in the warm breeze as the lights came on in the high-rises like a sky full of stars. The sea lapped gently against the sand in its rhythmic pulse, withdrawing.

Jennifer took Christine's hand and, startled, Christine flinched, then relaxed.

"I'm glad we came, Mother," Jennifer said.

"I am too," Christine said.

It was amazing, Christine thought, how your child's approval could mean so much. Once, before a piano recital—Jennifer was thirteen, the youngest participant—

Christine had noticed a large iridescent bug crawling on the white collar of one of the other girls' dresses. "You don't want this here, do you?" she laughed, and removed the bug, taking it to the window to release it without killing it, as Jennifer would have insisted.

The recital was rather indifferent, but Jennifer performed beautifully, Christine thought, and a thrill of exultation whelmed in her as she envisioned taking her daughter in her arms and telling her how much she loved her. But when the applause died at the end of the recital, Jennifer fled the room, her face red with rage or embarrassment.

When Christine finally caught up with her outside, Jennifer was wailing, "Mother, how could you, how could you?"

"What are you talking about?" Christine said.

"Everyone was asking who that crazy woman was, and it was *you, my* mother."

"What?"

"The bug," Jennifer said. "Why did you have to point out that bug? What an awful thing to do to me. I'm so embarrassed, so embarrassed!"

Christine had looked at her daughter helplessly. What would a profession of love mean now? They drove home in silence, Jennifer hugging the car door, all of Christine's longings left unsung.

The tide slipped in around their feet, and withdrew.

"I'm glad we came here, Mother," Jennifer said again. "Despite Douglas."

"I don't know how she can live with him," Christine said. "He's so, so ..."

"Insufferable?"

"Yes. Pompous. He never listens."

"I guess she loves him," Jennifer said.

"I just can't imagine," Christine said.

They walked on in silence, the sea advancing, withdrawing.

"Mother," Jennifer finally said, dropping her hand, "You always said I could do anything I wanted to, be anybody I wanted to be. That I should be the boss of things. I'm seventeen and I need my own life. Mother, I've decided ... I'm ... moving out." She said the words haltingly, but quietly. Blunt knives. "Dad agrees."

Christine stopped, started to say something, and then considered. "Where would you stay?" she said, fumbling for some neutral response, buying time to think.

"With Lydia."

The sun had set, and the moon was a lozenge on the lip of the coastline. In the half-light Jennifer looked somehow peaceful, as if the announcement had freed her.

"I like Lydia a lot," Jennifer said. "I ... love Lydia."

A woman's scream rang out from one of the condo garages set back off the beach. And then a series of screams, inhuman, like an animal in pain. A car door slammed—or perhaps it was a shot—and somebody shouted down from a window. "Hey, what's going on out there?"

The screams subsided, and there was the sound of a scuffle, a trash can, perhaps, turned over, and then another car door.

"What was that!" Christine said, and started off in the direction of the commotion.

"Don't, Mother," Jennifer called after her. "Leave it alone. It's not your business. Don't get involved. *Please*, there's nothing you can do."

wrestling

"have you thought about your wardrobe yet?" she says.

"My *what?*" I reply, pinning her arm behind her back.

"Your wardrobe," she says. She grabs my hair and pulls hard. "When I went off on my own, to college, I remember how I coordinated my skirts and blouses and shoes. My shoes were gray and brown and blue and pink so they would go with anything."

I have her in a half nelson now. "Don't worry about me," I say.

She slams me into the corner cupboard and kicks her heel into my shin. "And what about this vegetarian diet of yours? How will you get enough protein?"

As the pain shoots through my kneecap I pull her to the ground. I could comment on her peacock blue polyester pantsuit, or the cows she murders for meat, but I don't. I get her in a hammerlock. "I guess I'm going to miss you," I say, with only the slightest tinge of irony.

I've almost got her pinned, but she manages to wrench over onto her stomach. "You probably won't be calling home much, either, I suppose."

Somehow she's managed to flip me and I'm straining under her weight. "Just let go, why don't you?" I grimace.

She gets me in a scissors grip, and squeezes. "I know, you're on your own now, dear. I know."

I'm breathing hard, confused by her sudden maneuver. I can see God's hand hovering above the mat as my shoulders arch and twist. The crowd hoots and whistles. I'm down, but I'm not out. In my corner, the future is waving, shouting its loud instructions. I know what I have to do.

"I love you," I tell her. "I love you."

And she's down for the count.

siding

"You ain't got no vapor barrier in the house," the fat tin man wheezes. "That's what makes all your paint pop off. Now aluminum," he sings, "aluminum …"

The wife knows this song by heart, her song—the fascia and soffits and weep holes, the Styrofoam insulation, the window wraps and tracks. The stereo booms from the living room. "Just can it," she yells at their teenage daughter, her ears caulked with rock music.

"It's guaranteed," the tin man intones, "for life."

The husband isn't so sure. He thinks it's a surface problem—bad preparation, warped boards, cheap paint. He kicks at the family cat who yowls tinnily and bares her rotting teeth.

The tin man agrees, but says stripping down to bare wood is a bitch, and possibly an environmental hazard. Again, he counsels replacement.

siding

The daughter, thin as a paint chip, wired to her walkman, scrapes the cat off the floor and peals out of the house, siding with no one.

The tin man continues—no rotting, no peeling, no blistering: a new start.

The wife likes the idea and picks and picks at the paint.

"Don't!" the husband commands her, watching his whole house flake slowly away, his old angers condensing, his face moist, his passion stirring.

His voice is as insidious as mildew, the wife thinks, lifting her hand like a barrier, her skin a nest of ants, her smile a stain on her face.

The tin man comes between them with his lifetime guarantee.

But things are getting steamy now. "Who asked you?" they say, cutting him off, nailing him firmly in place.

worry

She worried about people; he worried about things. And between them, that about covered it.

"What would you think of our daughter sleeping around?" she said.

"The porch steps are rotting," he replied. "Someone's going to fall through."

They were lying in bed together, talking. They had been lying in bed together talking these twenty-five years: first, about whether to have children—she wanted to (although there was Downs' Syndrome, leukemia, microcephalia, mumps); he didn't (the siding was warped; the roof was going fast)—and then, after their daughter was born, a healthy seven pounds eleven ounces ("She's not eating enough"; "The furnace is failing"), about family matters, mostly ("Her friends are hoodlums, her room is a disaster"; "The brakes are squealing, the water heater's rusting out").

worry

Worry grew between them like a son, with his own small insistencies and then more pressing demands. They stroked and coddled him; they set a place for him at the table; they sent him to kindergarten, private school, and college. Because he failed at nearly everything and always returned home, they loved him. After all, he was their son.

"I've been reading her diary. She does drugs. She sleeps around."

"I just don't think I can fix them myself. Where will we find a carpenter?"

And so it went. Their daughter married her high school sweetheart, had a family, and started a health food store in a distant town. Although she recalled her childhood as fondly as anyone—how good her parents had been and how they worried for her, how old and infirm they must be growing, their house going to ruin—she rarely called or visited. She had worries of her own.

topless in tucson

He met her in a topless bar in Tucson. He'd spent the day, the last day of his Southwestern trip, hiking in the Saguaro National Monument East and Sabino Canyon, observing the ocotillos with their improbably erotic arms tipped with blaze orange blooms; the acacia, lush, sun-like, exuberant; the hopeful patches of daisy fleabane; the palo verde with its smooth green skin. It was beautiful, he thought, in its own way. Stark, still, the steady wind with nothing much to blow through to make sound, the occasional ratchet of a flicker or woodpecker on a saguaro, the chitter of a cactus wren, a lone lizard scurrying across the sand. Though, next to the lush green he was used to back home, there was also something shabby in the landscape—the wounded saguaros, blasted by potshots; the lop-eared prickly pears; the hard-scrabble barren patches littered with mesquite, ironwood, and sage.

He was trying not to think about his wife, his daughters off at college at Duke and Kalamazoo, the decisions he'd planned to make out in the desert. Could they, after twenty-five years of marriage, finally call it quits, sell the house and country property, divvy up the spoils, and go their separate ways? His daughters wouldn't understand—they seemed to be oblivious to the fact that for years things hadn't been going particularly well. The disagreements about money (she wanted to spend it; he didn't), about sex (he wanted to have it; she didn't), about their daughters (she was a strict disciplinarian; he, a libertarian), about work (for years, he did too much of it; and now that he had slowed down, she, with her recent promotion, did too much). Without the children in the house they'd found they had little left in common, and little more than inertia to keep them going.

And so, they'd decided to take separate vacations—he, by himself, to the Southwest, a part of the country he'd never seen; she, with her old college roommate, to New Orleans to eat Creole and make the jazz scene. When they returned, they'd have a long talk about the future. It wasn't his idea. He'd have preferred to coast along, pretending that everything was fine, and slide gracefully, if uneventfully, into old age. She believed in conflict and change, that sudden disruptions were good; that rage, released, was fertile and invigorating; that rage, repressed, was deadening and destructive. And so, he'd agreed to go, although he wasn't at all sure what he'd do alone.

He flew to Phoenix, stayed in the Radisson Tempe Mission Palms Hotel, cruised the upscale coffeehouses on Mill Street with their college clientele, drove into the Superstitions with their bald hills and hippies, watched pornographic videos on his pay-per-view TV. He went to the Grand Canyon, stayed in El Tovar with its dark carpets and heavy mahogany woodwork and massive lobby hearth; he hiked down onto Tonto Plain, through two million years of geologic history, redbuds spraying from crevices, cottonwoods at Indian Gardens blowing their fluff in his face, and stopped in the cool April sun to watch the tiny rafts plunge through the rapids down below and out of view.

He drove through Sedona with its red cliffs and fake Spanish shopping mall, feeling lonely and wondering what he was doing there. He did love his wife, he thought, at least when he was away from her. He did miss her. The world was made for couples, he thought, as he watched his fellow travelers, in twos and threes, laughing in restaurants, directing each other to beautiful views, consulting on possible purchases. Was it just his imagination that restaurant hostesses looked at him askance, disgusted that he'd be taking up an entire table? The low point had been, he thought, that first day when he'd hovered outside the Taco Bell in Tempe, hungry, but finally not gone in, afraid that, after he ordered, food in hand, there might be no empty tables. Had he been with Christine, he'd have marched right in. How had he grown so dependent on her?

So, when, on his long last day hiking thirteen miles through the ninety-five degree desert heat, tired and thirsty, he saw the sign on the outskirts of Tucson, in capital letters atop a narrow flat-roofed building, "TOPLESS IN TUCSON," he pulled his rental car off of Speedway, parked, and boldly walked in.

He had never been in such an establishment before. Although they existed at home, he had always been afraid that he might run into a colleague or student, and so, although he was curious, he'd never stopped. Back in junior high school—was it forty years ago?—in St. Louis he had sneaked downtown on the streetcar with Jerry Chalmers, a loud-mouthed kid who could talk for both of them, to the World Burlesque Theatre—"Live, No Movies"—where, despite his visible terror and the bouncer's glare, the manager waved them on in. He had seen Evelyn West, with her "$50,000 treasure chest, as insured by Lloyd's of London"; Candi Barr, "as good as her name"; and a couple of old vaudeville comics ("Doctor, Doctor, take my temperature. Doctor, Doctor, I didn't know thermometers were so big!" "You know how the Fugarwee Indians got their name? They were nomads and every morning they woke up in a strange place and said, 'Where the fugarwee?'") The theater was on its last legs, the seats broken, the fabric stained and torn, the audience composed of a couple of sailors, a fat woman, and an old wino who masturbated into a cup halfway through the performance and moaned audibly.

But this bar was different. It was a hot day for April, still at least ninety degrees, and the doors were opened wide to the air, rock music pulsing out into the small parking lot. When he stepped in out of the glare, the dark momentarily overcame him, and, blind, he felt his way along the wall to the first two-person table with its tall bar stools, and slipped in.

In the middle of the bar two stages were bathed in light, while tables receded off into the darkness. The walls were mirrored, giving the illusion of an enormous interior. He couldn't tell for sure at first whether there were actually two stages, or whether the second was just a reflection, but as the voice on the PA system announced "a doubles dance—Jackie and Linda!" he began to make things out more clearly.

There were two rooms, about the same size, with tables arranged along the edges, and each had a round bar area with a stage in the middle. Jackie—or was it Linda?—swept up the steps to the stage, behind his bar. She was young, early twenties perhaps, and thin. For the first dance she stayed clothed in a translucent tunic that revealed a thong bikini underneath. For the second dance she removed the tunic and bikini top. She was so flat-chested that he wondered whether she was possibly a man—but no, she was too delicate, he decided.

As he watched her and the other girls that roamed around the room stopping at tables to chat with the clientele, he was reminded of his daughters, a comparison that doused whatever eroticism the scene might otherwise have provoked. Yes, they were all young enough to be his daughters. The girl on stage was now writhing on the floor, simulating intercourse, moving her body more or less to the beat, and leering at the spectators in the way that some women think men think is sexy. He looked away.

At a nearby table a dancer was removing her blouse and dancing privately for the patron, a young man in a baseball cap whose confident smile suggested that he was no stranger to the bar. There was something different about this dancer. She moved with more grace, and her body had a soft maturity that was missing in the other girls. She was topless now, with black fishnet stockings over red bikini bottoms. What was it about her? A calm, an unself-consciousness, a serenity—yes, that was it. There was a serenity about her, as if she were dancing for herself and not for the patron or him or anyone else. She seemed oblivious to everything in the room but herself and the music, and she flowed like a willow, like music, like water. As he gazed at her, transfixed, she glanced up and seemed to smile at him. He smiled and involuntarily nodded.

A hand touched his shoulder. "Hi. How are you tonight?" a voice asked. Standing next to him was a young woman, maybe twenty-two, with a slightly foreign look, Middle Eastern perhaps, in black panties and halter top.

"That's my girlfriend up there," she said, pointing to the blonde on the stage. "This is her first night. I encouraged her to come. She's very nervous. Maybe you could tip her, make her feel better."

He hadn't noticed the new girl on the stage. She was statuesque, pretty in a brittle sort of way, with high cheekbones and lots of makeup. She did seem nervous. He wondered, however, whether this was a con and he was the mark. Maybe every night the girl at his side roamed the tables rousing sympathy for various dancers.

"I'm nervous, too," he joked. "My first time in a topless bar. What do I do?"

"Really," she said, looking him in the eye. "Well, you just step over to the bar and slip a dollar bill into her G-string. No touching. And she'll dance a little bit just for you."

He looked past her toward the patron across the room. "I saw a girl dancing at a table, over there." He motioned quizzically.

"Oh," she said. "A table dance. Here." She stepped in front of him and grabbed his crossed knee. "Spread your legs."

Her familiarity took him by surprise, and he remained rigid.

"Loosen up," she said, and pulled his knee down. "You spread your legs and I dance between them like this," she swayed seductively. "Up close and personal," she said.

He handed her a dollar bill. "Thanks for the information," he said.

"Is this to make me go away? Or to make me stay and talk to you?"

He wondered if he had insulted her. "Thanks, really," he said, and she moved off to another table.

He ducked over to the bar, waited until the dancer paused over him and slipped a dollar bill into her G-string. She shook her breasts appreciatively in his face and then resumed her dance.

He settled back into his seat against the wall. It certainly wasn't PC, he thought. His female colleagues would be appalled. His daughters would be appalled. His wife would be appalled. Exploitation and abuse. And yet, it was pleasant, watching the girls robe and disrobe, dance and defer to him. It wasn't really erotic or arousing. It just seemed natural to have beautiful women around. If anything, he rationalized, they seemed less abused and exploited than the waitresses who, fully clothed, ranged from table to table with their precarious trays, or the young women he had seen earlier on the trail crew hauling rocks and jackhammering steps into the hillside.

"Would you like a table dance?"

He looked up to see the woman who had been dancing at the next table standing beside him, a gauzy chemise covering her to her thighs. Her voice was lyrical, musical, and the question was neither provocative nor businesslike. It seemed merely friendly, generous, natural, like a hostess at a small party saying, "Would you care for a glass of water?" Or, "Is there anything I can get you?" She smiled at him, a pleasant, neutral smile, as if she were just happy to be there with him.

"That would be nice," he said, and spread his legs.

She moved in close and shimmied her chemise over her head, swaying slowly. She certainly had a beautiful body, he thought. Not thin, but not heavy. Healthy. Mature. She looked directly at him as she danced, her smile relaxed and genuine.

"I was watching you over there," he said.

"I was watching *you,*" she said.

Another scripted remark, he thought, but he didn't care.

"I'm forty-four," she said. "I've been doing this for over twenty years."

He smiled. "That must be why I like you," he said. "The other girls are too young."

His hands clasped in his lap, he noticed his wedding ring. Perhaps he should have taken it off, but she didn't seem to notice.

"It's a better job than most," she said. "I make good money. I'm putting myself through school. I'm studying to be an RN." She swayed calmly, serenely before him.

He'd probably had too much to drink, the waitress continually stopping by to bring him another schooner of beer. Awkward as a teenager, he mumbled something about his hike in the desert.

She seemed genuinely interested. "Oh, good for you," she said. "I biked up the Sabino Canyon Road once. You can imagine, it was quite a trip. Coming down was a lot easier."

Was she married? Did she have kids? Who were her friends? He didn't ask.

"You make dancing look like fun," he said.

"It is. It is fun. I work when I want to, take off when I want to. And when I walk out of here, I'm just like anyone else. They don't pay us, you know. We work for tips. But the tips are good."

The music ended, and she slipped on her chemise.

"How much for the dance?" he asked.

"Five dollars."

"How about twenty," he said.

She seemed momentarily confused. "Twenty for the one dance, and nothing else?"

"Twenty for the one dance. It was worth it," he said.

"Well, thank you," she said, and lingered at his table. The man in the baseball cap motioned to her.

"I have to go," she said. "Is that all right?"

"Sure," he said. "But come back later."

She did come back later and dance another table dance, and then another, for which he paid her another forty dollars, and then she stayed and talked for half an hour. "My break," she said. She told him how she had moved to Arizona from Chicago with her parents when she was ten and never left, how her friends tended to be the dancers and the students who kept getting younger and younger, how she didn't know whether she would really like nursing, how she did really like to dance and could make $20,000 to $25,000 per year working evenings. How her name was Melissa, but everyone called her Lissa.

And did he tell her about how, after a day of seeing beautiful exotic things with beautiful exotic names—saguaros, ocotillos, boojums, acacias, palo verde trees—

here he was seeing the most beautiful and exotic thing of all? Or about his wife and daughters, about how he was contemplating a separation, about his life in the history department, how he cherished rare things, how she was a rare thing, how he felt blessed in spending this time with her? Later he would remember the evening as romantic, generous, expansive. Or was he simply drunk and tongue-tied, trying to shout banalities over the rock music?

She did one last table dance for him and then he left, walked out tipsy into the warm night and the vast Southwestern sky.

By the time the plane landed, he had begun to look forward to seeing Christine. Lissa was a lovely dream, but he was ready to get on with his life, which wasn't, after all, he thought, so bad. Out the window of the plane he could see the gray day, a light rain falling on the shabby grass, the trees still stark and black, the remains of winter littering the runway.

His wife was not at the gate as she'd promised. While other people were being met with joyful hugs and exclamations, he searched for her in the crowd and then proceeded down the escalator to the ground floor. She was always late. He shouldn't have expected her to meet him, he supposed. That was one of the things they had always argued about. He wanted to be early for movies, to get a good seat and be sure he didn't miss anything. She wanted to arrive just as the feature was starting so as not to waste time sitting in the theater. For popular first-run movies they often ended up in the front row, all other seats taken, staring at gigantic blurry heads on the screen. The same was true of plays and concerts and parties. She would never start getting ready until it was time to leave, and then she would run the water in the bathtub to shave her legs, or stand at her closet trying on outfit after outfit, unable to find just the right thing, while he waited, impatient in the car.

Now he stood downstairs beside the ticket counter, watching both lobby doors. Perhaps she had forgotten, and he should phone her? As he was deciding what to do, she burst through the sliding door and caught sight of him.

"I *am* sorry," she said. "I was grocery shopping and the line took forever." She kissed him briefly, and he noticed the faint aroma of garlic that had grown so familiar.

On the drive home she bubbled about her trip to New Orleans, how great the music was, how he would have loved it, how some man had tried to pick her up at their hotel, how the restaurants were superb. He found himself growing gloomier and gloomier, and when she asked him how Arizona was, he gave only a curt reply. He was tired, he said. It had been a long flight. She understood, she said. But it was so good to see him. She had missed him. She knew he hadn't wanted to go, hadn't doubted their relationship. The vacation was just what she needed. How could she have thought that they should consider a separation? Everything would be better from here on in. She was sure of it.

He found it hard to get back in his old routine. Sitting in his office at the college, consulting with colleagues, handling correspondence, he daydreamed about Lissa. Lying awake in bed at night, Christine already asleep, her back turned to him as usual, he dreamed about Lissa. As Christine slipped contentedly back into the long days at work, dinner in front of "The Lehrer News Hour", the occasional collegial cocktail party, their parallel but separate lives, it obsessed him—this image of ocotillos, saguaros, acacias, sunshine, desert, and Lissa, topless in her black mesh tights, smiling her serene, sweet smile as she danced just beyond his reach.

And then he got the letter. In his departmental mailbox, mixed in with the ads for new books, the announcements of conferences, the fliers about computer upgrade classes, there it was, a lavender envelope with lyrical flowing script, and a return address in Tucson. He closed his office door and opened the envelope. It was from Lissa—a breezy letter about her nursing classes, the biking she'd been doing in the desert, the weather—as if they'd been friends all their lives. The letter closed with the simple admonition: "Write me." She signed it "Topless in Tucson." He found himself short of breath, trembling. Here he was, fifty-five years old, a full professor, and trembling over a letter.

The departmental secretary tapped on the door and entered. He looked up at her, or somewhere past her.

"Sorry," she began. "I've got a problem with ..." She hesitated. "Are you all right?"

"Oh. Yes," he replied. "I'm fine, fine. Just distracted for a moment. What's the problem?"

They corresponded weekly—friendly letters; they were pen pals, nothing more. He found himself looking forward to the mail every Wednesday—an account of her week, the most trivial things possessing a magic: what she had for dinner, how her cat was eating her plants, some item of clothing she had purchased. And he found himself spending the better part of the afternoon writing back, about his work (something Christine had never seemed particularly interested in), how his daughters were doing in school, the conflicts he had with his wife. They were like good friends, brother and sister perhaps, and he began to feel closer to her than he had felt to anyone in a long time.

When she invited him to meet her somewhere—he could pick the place, just a day or two, she said, like that Alan Alda movie, one of her favorites, maybe they could just meet one day each year, no one would have to know—he felt a momentary excitement, and then dread. The letters had been exhilarating, had provided the thrill of the off-limits and dangerous. But did he really want to see her? He slipped the letter into his briefcase and went home.

That night Christine went to bed early with a headache, and he stayed up to watch *The Blue Angel* on TV. A gruff and staid professor who had never really lived, never had a passion for anything except for classroom order and his books, meets a beautiful dance hall "artiste" and falls in love—with her youth, her vitality, her utter unfamiliarity.

She, meanwhile, accustomed to the false glamour, the adoring fans, the seedy surroundings, sees in him the possibility of a higher life, of being valued for her intellect, her generosity, her self, not her body and her persona. The professor's improbable devotion to her costs him his teaching post, but the two marry and are, at first, perfectly happy.

As time passes, however, her youth and his age, her openness and his repression, her flirtations and his fastidiousness, collide. He is reduced to peddling cheesecake photographs of her, and she comes to despise him. In the end, when the troupe returns to his hometown, he is forced to play the magician's clown assistant. In his phony nose and fright wig, an egg cracked on his head, he crows like a rooster, a crow that at the beginning of the marriage represented triumph but now has become a cry of anguish and utter despair for his lost life and his lost love.

When he slid into bed, his heart still half in the movie, he saw that Christine was crying.

"What's wrong," he said.

She didn't answer.

"Christine?" he said.

As she lay there, her back turned to him, sobbing now, he felt a tenderness for her that he had not felt for years. They had had a good life together, he thought. And it was comfortable, and safe. What had he been thinking? Had he really wanted to take that kind of risk? He hadn't wanted to hurt Christine. And there were his daughters to think about, his position at the college. What sort of absurd fantasy had he been living in? He had only spent two hours with Lissa, and, despite all the letters, what did he really know about her? She was a forty-four-year-old stripper. That was all.

"Christine," he said again. "I'm sorry."

She was silent now. And then, "It's not you," she said. "It's me. It's us. Let's never throw away what we've got. Can you forgive me?" she said. And then she told him about the man in New Orleans.

It had stunned and confused him, her revelation. And it had hurt him more deeply than he might have imagined. He didn't tell her about Lissa—what was there, after all, to tell? His lapse seemed so innocent next to her transgression. Or was his worse? Hers had been just a brief fling, a weekend affair. His had gone on for months as he embroidered romantic fantasies around it.

After his initial shock and humiliation, his feelings of betrayal and inadequacy, anger had set in. He would be justified now, he thought, in meeting Lissa somewhere. It would serve Christine right. But anger quickly turned into sorrow, a sense of loss, and, finally, a numb self-pity. It just no longer seemed worth all the effort.

He stopped writing to Lissa. Her letters appeared faithfully for several weeks, and he slipped them, unopened, into the recycling bin with the junk mail. And then the letters stopped.

Then, one day in late September when he picked up his office phone, it was Lissa.

"Hello," she said. Her voice was as musical as he remembered it—calm, like a glass of cool water. "You stopped writing me. I thought maybe something had happened. Are you all right?"

"Lissa," he said, and stopped.

"I wasn't asking you to leave your wife or anything," she said. "I just like being pen pals. I just thought we could meet once a year and not tell anybody. It would be our secret. If we could meet just once a year, for a beautiful weekend, that would be enough. Hey, I hardly remember what you look like. Maybe we'd meet once and never want to meet again. Who knows?"

"We can't," he said.

"Look," she said. "I'm coming up North. Don't worry. I won't look for you. I'm visiting a friend. She's a dancer at Mr. G's. Do you know it? She got me a gig to pay for the trip. I'll be dancing every night for two weeks. Come see me," she said.

The Thursday before the weekend that Lissa had said she would be at Mr. G's, Christine was out at her book group and he was home alone. He flipped on the TV, surfing around the dial with the remote. He flipped past a program on the Discovery Channel and then flipped back. It was a nature show on life in the desert, how what seemed an inhospitable, dead place was really alive with plants and animals. There were panoramas of cactus fields and brief portraits of the desert creatures—packrats, lizards, tarantulas, jays, flickers, wrens, and the twenty-seven varieties of rattlesnake, which, the program insisted, were unjustly feared. There were pictures of the monsoons in August, when flash floods left the desert floor glistening and lush, the bright air filled with the sound of birdsong and thirsty succulents. Yes, he thought. He would see her. He would find some excuse to leave the house tomorrow night and see her. He flipped off the TV and went to bed.

When Christine came home just after midnight, he feigned sleep. In the moonlight she seemed insubstantial as a dream, her bare arms and face alabaster, evanescent. She glided past the bed and paused, but when he didn't stir, she continued on into the attached dressing room. They had used it, years ago, as a nursery for their daughters, and it still contained a crib folded in the closet, along with some games and toys ("for the grandchildren, one day," she'd said), the detritus of their long years together. She unbuttoned her dress and draped it over the chair, and, dressed only in her silk half-slip, stood silent before the full-length mirror.

    He watched her as she began to sway, almost imperceptibly, as if to some unheard music, her small breasts glowing in the moonlight. Another man had seduced her! he thought. Or she had seduced him. The horror and the wonder of it! How had he not noticed, lately, that she still retained much of her youthful beauty? She began to hum, tunelessly, and then to sway more visibly, oblivious to him, dancing now with her reflection, shimmering like moonlight on broken water, like prairie grasses, like wheat. What was there about long marriage that exposed it all—the scars, the warts, the boredom—but let him see her now, in the mirror of desire and contentment, a mystery, an enigma, more precious for the confidences they'd keep?

    He watched her and her reflection as they danced together, rhythmic, serene, like willows, like bloodroot, like trillium, her pale skin cool and lovely in the moonlight, closer now, before him, like snowmelt after the long Midwestern winter.

quick bright things

He couldn't shake it, this feeling that they were all going to die. It had come to him unexpectedly, unbidden, in a sudden flash of vision, or insight, as he was preparing his annual lecture on the causes of the Vietnam War, in which he showed how the United States had, with the very best intentions, come to the aid of the French in the 1950s, totally ignorant of the Vietnamese people's history or culture. What was current events for Peterson was ancient history for his students who had been infants when the war finally ended. He remembered that day vividly, driving home from town to Christine, hearing on the car radio the announcement that the war was officially over. It was as if a weight had been lifted from him. If this war, this endless war, could be over, so could his conflicts with Christine.

But it meant nothing to his current students, who seemed more interested in getting the highest grades with the least work so they could go on to get their M.B.A.s and earn the most money. Maybe he could make some connection between the current crisis in the Middle East, maybe he could get them to see how they could all learn something from the lessons of history.

His thoughts drifted to Christine and Jennifer and Phoebe, how much he missed them after only a few days. They had gone to visit Christine's parents in Milwaukee for the long weekend and were due back this evening. Peterson hadn't wanted to go—he had never liked Christine's father—so he pulled out the old excuse of work and drove himself out to their country place. It had been pleasant—the seclusion, the quiet, the freedom to work on his lectures in peace. But this morning he'd woken up with a pain in his chest, indigestion he figured, and all day he had been uneasy, plagued with some inexplicable emptiness or dread.

Halfway into his lecture it hit him: they were all going to die—Christine, Jennifer, Phoebe. He saw them in the Neon, rounding the circle of Goodfellow Road and County Y in the blind spot where the town board had made a gravel cut years ago, Christine, as always, driving too fast, as a pickup truck of high school boys returning from Prairie Center slammed into them. The vision played itself over and over in his mind. It was absurd, he knew. But somehow, it was as real as if it had already happened. "So quick bright things come to confusion," he thought, remembering a line from Shakespeare.

He wished now that he had gone with them to Milwaukee. Christine would have preferred that, he knew, and he could have done the little work he had to do, there. He wished he'd told Christine and the girls he loved them before they left. He would tell them when they got back. Jennifer and Phoebe would be returning to college soon, summer vacation over, and he vowed to spend more time with them when they got back from Milwaukee.

If they got back, he found himself thinking again. He wouldn't get any more work done this day, he decided, not with that violent image pulsing before him. Maybe if he walked up to look at the cut, maybe if he ran the four-mile circle he hadn't run for years, he could shake off the anxiety that filled him like a canyon of regret. He put down his lecture, found a T-shirt, some shorts, and his old running shoes, and walked up the gravel road to the cut.

The intersection was well-marked, he noted, peaceful and deserted. It seemed impossible that anything could happen there, surrounded by the neatly grazed hillsides, the draws of cottonwoods and box elders. The corn, after a summer of plentiful rain and record-breaking temperatures, looked lush. At least they hadn't cut all the trees, he mused. And some scraggly vegetation now softened the stark limestone walls. The sun was high overhead, and it was almost unbearably hot. It had been over a hundred for three days straight, and it looked like it would be that again today. Perhaps he shouldn't run, after all.

He'd only run sporadically over the years; but he remembered now how settling running had been, how the repetitive rhythm of feet on pavement had always helped him think, had given him good ideas. Christine had worried about his heart, his high cholesterol. It was but another of the petty conflicts he wished he hadn't helped perpetuate.

He did some stretching exercises beside the road. He was in pretty good shape, he thought, for a man pushing sixty. Although he could no longer put his palms flat on the pavement, he could touch his toes with his fingertips, without straining his legs. "It's because your torso's so long, and your legs are so short," Christine had teased. "Why people value athletic ability so much, I'll never know," she had said.

    The wires on the power pole overhead hummed like bees, electrons surging in the transformer. He started at a slow pace up the narrow black-topped road, pleased at how much better he felt. The first fifty yards were uphill, and he negotiated the crest without getting at all winded. From the top of the ridge he could look out over the countryside across the fresh cut hay and alfalfa, the corn tassels patterning the land like wide-wale corduroy or herringbone as Christine had once said, to the steeple of the Catholic church—the halfway point on the four-mile circle—and then to the ridges and hills even further off in the distance. The immensity of the view had always surprised him, the blue sky stretching for miles, the sense of peacefulness and well-being that unbroken landscape provided. This was why he had bought the property in the first place. Away from the claustrophobic city with its crowds, cars, noise, and social demands, its houses jostling each other for attention or looming over the superfluous sidewalks.

As he began the slow coast down the first long hill, he felt a slight pain in his lower back and the hint of a stitch in his left side. He remembered his high school track coach yelling, "Roll down those hills, Kingsley. Roll down them."

    He rolled down the hillside past Goff's farm. He remembered how Goff had insinuated himself into Peterson's barn, shed, and meadow, with his indirect aggression. "That's a nice pasture you got there," Goff would say. "A guy could put some heifers in that pasture. You gonna put any heifers in that pasture?" For some reason Peterson had always felt guilty that he wasn't farming. Although he didn't want heifers or hay or machinery on his place, he couldn't think of any good reason to tell Goff no. Just saying he didn't want them there, that he wanted an empty barn, shed, and pasture, seemed somehow unfriendly. If *he* wasn't going to use them for their intended purpose, why shouldn't Goff? He always agreed, and then spent days resenting the manipulation. He hadn't talked with Goff at all this season, and he wondered where Goff was keeping his heifers, his extra hay and equipment now?

A tan and white foal grazed beside its mother in Goff's field. Phoebe would like to see that, Peterson thought. Maybe she would see it from the car on the way home later. He imagined her excitedly running to the house to tell him all about it. They had called her "the finder"; she always managed to find things when no one else could— lost keys, money, morels. She was lucky, everyone said. She was always winning raffles, cake walks, coloring contests. She loved animals. Once, after a fight with him, she "ran away" for a day and a night to the tent Peterson had pitched in the woods at the end of their property. She was going to forage for a living, she said. They had just seen *A Midsummer Night's Dream* at a local outdoor theater, and she said she was going to live like Puck, or like a deer.

He kicked a piece of baling twine and continued downhill. They had called her "lucky," although she was the one who needed the bottle-thick glasses at age seven— Christine's legacy to her—and the headgear and braces at ten—Peterson's contribution. She got the nickname

"Bean" for her skinny body, her stick-like legs. But she was talented, Peterson thought, composing her own pieces on the violin, piano, and trombone. She had even won a city-wide song-writing contest once.

    The hill leveled out, and Peterson noticed that the diamond-shaped road sign, yellow with the silhouette of a cow walking into the road, was still there, a hole in the cow's ass where some waggish hunter had taken target practice. Cottonwoods and sumac clustered in the draw. The pain in Peterson's lower back sent an occasional pulse down his leg, and his side-stitch threatened to move up into his shoulder. "Run through that pain," his coach would have yelled at him. "Goddamn it, just run through it." He jogged on.

    If Phoebe had been the Puckish sprite, all angles and energy, Jennifer was the beauty. When she was born, the doctors had discovered that her head wasn't growing and concluded that she was microcephalic. Peterson remembered the strain on him and Christine, how he'd nearly had a breakdown, how they'd gone to Mexico to forget, how they'd mused about a future in which the doctors were wrong and Jennifer turned out not only to be normal, but beautiful and smart. "Not bad for a retarded kid," they'd imagined themselves saying. And then, the doctors were wrong, or perhaps Peterson's prayers to the gods were answered. For, shortly after the Mexico trip, Jennifer's head started growing and her development proceeded in textbook fashion from then on. She was living with her friend, Lydia, now, and was happier than he had ever seen her.

    The road turned uphill again. The sun, aslant over the trees, was already bubbling the asphalt as Peterson watched his feet plod uphill. The front of his T-shirt was drenched with sweat, and his breath was coming hard. He passed the old Thiessen place, where a large dog, chained to a makeshift house, barked at him, dancing to the end of its chain and back. Years ago he had gotten to know all the dogs on the route. He had carried a stick ever since the day Scout, Thiessen's beautiful springer spaniel, had broken free of his chain, scampered down to the road, barking, and made a pass at Peterson, biting him in the calf before he knew what had happened. It hadn't really hurt—"itched" might have been a better way to describe it. He felt the tickle of hair on his legs as he ran by, saw the flurry of tan and rust at his feet, and felt the itch as the dog retreated to its front stoop.

He had never particularly liked dogs, from the black cocker spaniel his father had brought home for him when he was five—a frantic dog that was always knocking him over in its enthusiasm—to the terrier he had hit accidentally in the jaw with a baseball bat as a teenager when the dog, chasing the pitched tennis ball, leapt up seemingly from nowhere. Peterson had carried the memory of that dog, jaw splintered, whimpering at his feet, with him for years, trying to persuade himself that it wasn't his fault.

When Thiessen's springer spaniel rushed him, he had felt a surge of terror and guilt, and kept running until he saw two streams of blood flowing from tooth marks on either side of his calf. He had reacted more with outrage than anything else. What right had that dog to bite him? He hadn't done anything to it. It was the same kind of outrage he'd felt when that gangly retarded fellow in town had thrown a cup of cold yogurt in his face as he and Christine were walking home one night when they were first married.

After Scout's bite, Christine had urged Peterson to get a tetanus shot and have the dog impounded, but he did neither. Driving to town for the shot seemed too time-consuming, and impounding the dog seemed unneighborly. He suspected that the neighboring farmers already resented his presence in the community —"the rich city guy who bought the old Goodfellow place," he imagined them saying. "No, he don't work none, far as I can see. Teaches at the college, or something."

As he passed the Thiessen place, a coonhound came up behind him, crisscrossing the ditch on his right. He wished he'd thought to bring a stick along, but the dog didn't seem particularly interested in him and just kept drifting lazily along in parallel, sniffing through the weeds. Peterson reached the crest of the hill and ran more easily along the gentle dips in the road that approached the Catholic church. He looked out over the hillsides, where gray and silver silos glinted in the sun, and Holsteins, black and white, grazed against the robin's-egg-blue sky. Somewhere over the next rill he could hear the roar of the huge ventilation fans in a cow barn and the motor of the vacuum milk tank puttering. Although the pain in his side had abated, the pain down his left leg had become a dull pulse, and both legs were beginning to feel a bit rubbery. Perhaps he would have to walk the last mile or so. He was running straight up and down now, taking inefficient little stutter steps. "Lean into it," his coach would have insisted. "Stretch out."

He took several deep long breaths, the smell of silage and manure assailing him. Several Holsteins looked up as he passed, and one calf followed him inside the electric fence on his left for a few dozen steps.

He could see the steeple clock on the Catholic church clearly now, its hands stuck permanently at twelve noon. He must be moving slow today, he thought. In the old days it was fifteen minutes exactly to the church. Today, by the church clock, it had taken two hours. At this point in the circle he remembered that he had inevitably found himself thinking about his father. Just when Peterson felt like walking, wondering what he was doing out in the hot sun running anyway, his T-shirt and shorts drenched with sweat, his legs weak, his side aching, his head pounding, he'd thought about his father sitting in his wheelchair, slumped over in the nursing home, his gold front tooth gleaming through the crack in his half-smile as Peterson appeared in the doorway. His father couldn't lift his head or move more than a finger, and would have given anything to be able to run as Peterson was—for a man who could feel nothing anymore, the side stitch, the rubbery legs, the sweat, the shortness of breath would have been an indescribable pleasure. Peterson's petty fatigue was nothing compared to his father's incapacity, and this thought spurred him on. At any moment, you could be paralyzed or dead. He quickened his pace, the adrenaline flowing almost as it had when he was sixteen, running cross-country in high school, his mother urging him on at the finish line with the coaches and other fathers, where his father should have been.

He rounded the top of the hill by the church, its stone face unchanged. His mother had joined a new church in Arizona where she and Eddie had purchased a condo. They played bridge and golf almost daily with their new friends in the congregation. Eddie had turned out to be a godsend for her, after Peterson's father died, and Peterson wished he had been more accepting of him in the first place. Peterson's hostility had distressed his mother unnecessarily, and it certainly hadn't done his dead father any good for Peterson to remain morally outraged by his mother's remarriage.

In fact, his father probably would have been happy just to know that she was happy. He'd always been a fairly selfless person, even in his illness, concerned more with the well-being of others than his own. Peterson remembered his father telling him how he had responded to a call in *Reader's Digest* for first-person stories on the topic, "How I Live with a Disability." They paid one thousand dollars. But it wasn't the money or the "fame" that might attend publication that interested him. He honestly believed that his account of his own experience with multiple sclerosis could help others. The article was never published; it remained a yellowing typescript neatly folded in his father's metal strongbox, where Peterson found it after his death.

A rustling in the grass at the side of the road brought him back. He glanced into the weeds, but his eyes were bleared with sweat, and he could see nothing. Years ago, he had fancied that such rustlings were snakes. This was probably no more a snake than that piece of rope with which his uncle Wilford had scared off the women at that family reunion. Wilford had died not long ago, Peterson had heard, in his fishing boat, adrift on a farmer's pond. His wife, Evelyn, had gone out looking for him late one evening when he didn't come home, and found him in the moonlight, his pole still in his hands, his line run all the way out as if he had finally hooked into something big. Now she lived with Peterson's aunt Martha, who had finally given up on men.

Peterson fought up the steep incline to the old Hubble place with its shabby asphalt siding, its rusted tin roof, its unmown weedy farmyard—all quack and burdock—its defunct gray windmill, its pile of trash. He had always been appalled at the way some of the farmers just dumped their trash into ditches and draws on their property, or piled it in the yard. But what were they supposed to do with it, he asked himself. He had always taken his trash surreptitiously to town and found a dumpster.

He remembered the Hubble's dog, Spike, how it had always chased after him for fifty yards or so, barking menacingly. Now, as he turned the sharp corner and began the long downhill before the last uphill section, he caught sight of another dog, much like Spike, bounding from behind an outbuilding. It was a mongrel, its black hair mangy and burr-ridden, the dirty scruff around its mouth shaggy and wet with saliva. It snapped at his legs and bottom, snarling, but then fell into place off to his side in front of the more docile brown coonhound that had been accompanying Peterson for some time. He supposed if they were planning to bite him, they would have done so by now, and he relaxed into a smoother downhill pace.

If the mongrel looked a lot like Spike, the coonhound was a dead ringer for one the children had brought home years ago. "It just followed us, Dad," they had said. "And I suppose you didn't encourage it?" he had replied. "No," they'd insisted. "Did you discourage it?" "Well, no," they admitted. Peterson had explained, somewhat abruptly, that the dog probably belonged to someone else, that they would be sorry to lose it. "You wouldn't want that?" he asked them. "No," they lowered their heads. Although it was getting dark, he'd insisted that they walk the dog back to the house where it had joined them. When, after an hour, they still hadn't returned, he drove off after them, half angry, half worried that something had happened. When he found them on the road, with the dog at their feet, they'd explained that no one was home, and every time they tried to leave, the dog followed them. Phoebe was in tears. "We knew you'd get mad," she said, "if we brought the dog home again."

The pain had become fairly constant in Peterson's left side now, and he was running, even downhill, with a slight limp. He would stop soon and walk, he told himself, taking several deep breaths. A strong smell in the air assailed him, the smell of alfalfa and cows, yes, but some other smell he hadn't experienced for some time, a sweet, but rank smell, a musky, slightly sour, overpowering odor, the odor, he realized, of something dead. The coonhound wandered off in the weeds to investigate. These were the August days, Peterson recalled, when families of raccoons and possums chose to cross the roads, their bodies flattened and fly-ridden. Phoebe, he remembered, was horrified by the deaths of animals. People never affected her quite as much, but an animal, dead on the road or in a book or a movie, could make her weep inconsolably. He was always careful to misdirect her. When she'd see something in the road from the car, he'd assure her that it was just trash, a paper bag, something that had dropped from a farmer's truck.

Three crows rose flapping from the weeds as the coonhound continued circling. Peterson remembered a conversation he had had with Jennifer. Out of the blue one day she'd said, "You know, it's a good thing people die."

"Oh, why is that?" Peterson had asked.

"Well, it gives you a reason to do things. If you were going to live forever, why would you do anything?"

"If you're just going to die anyway," Peterson had baited her, "why bother?"

"Everybody has something to accomplish. Some contribution, some things you need to do. Death gives them some urgency."

Not a bad little philosopher, Peterson had told Christine later. Not bad for a retarded kid.

He was running on the valley floor now, through bottom land, flat and even. Some of the pain had gone, and he could see the shade up ahead where the long final hill began. Maybe he could run the whole way after all, he thought. He coasted along the road. *Everybody has something to accomplish. Some contribution.* What had been his contribution? The past few years seemed a blur of sameness—the history courses which he knew by heart, the yellowing lectures he swore as a young professor he'd never resort to, the withdrawal gradually from departmental affairs as younger colleagues implemented changes in committee organization and degree programs, the migration of his friends to better paying positions at more prestigious universities, the failure to finish the books he had once hoped would make his reputation.

Oh, there had been some high points—the first few years of teaching, the publication of a few dozen articles and poems, the citation for excellence in service to the college. But the older he got, the less interested he was in his career.

And then, of course, there was Lissa....

He passed into the shade at the bottom of the long hill. It was the first shade he'd encountered on the whole run, and it eased him somewhat. The whole hillside was in shadow, the sun having dropped behind the steep, treed bluff. It was cooler in the shade and he welcomed it, although the hill would be difficult and long. Staring at the pavement now, pushing himself to get up the long last hill, he heard the chirr of crickets and locusts, and saw the sulphur and cabbage butterflies massing in the cracked asphalt at his feet.

The white indentation of a tooth mark was still visible on the inside of his calf as he forced his legs up the hill. He remembered his outrage years ago as Scout scampered back to the porch yapping. It had taken old man Thiessen a few minutes to notice Peterson out front shouting and pointing. Peterson wasn't about to leave without letting Thiessen know what had happened, but he couldn't approach the house with Scout stationed in the way. When Thiessen finally saw him, he insisted that Peterson come in, have the wound treated, and have some breakfast. Thiessen was seventy and hard of hearing; he apologized to Peterson as he shakily applied some Merthiolate and tried unsuccessfully to get a Band-Aid to stick to Peterson's sweaty leg until Peterson finally dissuaded him. Peterson had ended up staying so long to talk with him that Christine began to worry and came looking. "I thought you'd had a heart attack for sure," she told him later.

He still had two scars from that bite. He remembered a storyteller who had visited his third grade class—was it nearly fifty years ago?—and told stories about some of his scars. The storyteller then had the children tell stories about *their* scars. When it got to Peterson, he had no scars to tell about. After school, he'd run home to his mother, feeling embarrassed and deprived. "Don't worry," she'd told him. "You'll have your scars to tell about soon enough."

He passed a road sign that had always amused him—STEEP, WINDING CURVE, 15 MPH—and joked aloud that he guessed he'd have to speed up. He was running so slow now that it was more like a walk, a slow-motion pantomime of running, as if the pavement were moving steadily away from him with each step he took, his feet barely able to lift themselves under his body to keep it from falling. He was almost back to the house now, though, just half of the long hill to go. He thought of Jennifer and Phoebe playing badminton, Christine humming at her loom, the goats clattering on the oak platform he'd built for them in the pen he'd constructed out of old gates he'd found around the farm, the chickens poking through the new mown grass for insects and scraps. He thought he could hear a dove cooing in the box elders, a phoebe calling its name from a fence post, a bevy of goldfinches ringing their tiny bells high on the wires.

The cool breeze in the ridge's shadow chilled him, a shiver that started at the nape of his neck where his wet hair dripped, and trickled down his spine, wrapping itself in tiny rivulets around his ribs and chest. And then the rivulets were thin arms squeezing gently, pushing him toward the unmowed roadside weeds, his legs and thighs trembling with the unending incline, as he thought, *yes, a rest wouldn't be such a bad idea, yes, just a few moments in the weeds, yes,* as he stumbled into the Queen Anne's lace and chicory, the ragweed and wild mustard, the goldenrod and coneflower, and collapsed, dizzily wheezing. It was peaceful in the weeds, a few bees humming, three dogs circling, a cardinal red in the trees.

He remembered stories of Goff's wild dogs, how they roamed the woods, attacking deer and cattle. He had heard their ghostly yelping across the hills on starry evenings, the full moon illuminating the farmyard with milky light. Now the mongrel that had followed him loomed lean and ominous, teeth bared, mangy face thrust in his face. "Spike," he heard himself say. "Spike." Now Spike was licking his cold forehead and cheeks, the dog's rough tongue soothing as a massage. Now the brown coonhound had joined him, and other dogs gathered around, cooing and warbling.

Christine would find him. She'd arrive home to an empty house, begin to worry, and bring the car around. She'd chastise him for pushing himself too hard. "What a foolish thing to do," she'd say. Off through the fillips of Queen Anne's lace and chicory, he thought he could hear Phoebe and Jennifer singing in the breeze. And was that Christine singing, too? They had always made such wonderful spontaneous harmony. So *quick bright things*, he thought. So *quick bright things*. Now all the dogs in the neighborhood were gathered, like Theseus' musical hounds, yipping, yapping, and yodeling in unison some familiar tune. Now a howl, now a croon, now a moan. Now the Queen Anne's lace and chicory. Now the wind without measure or sound.

acknowledgments

The stories in this collection were originally published in the following publications: *The Alaska Quarterly Review*, "The Little Woman"; *Beloit Fiction Journal*, "The Quarry," "Topless in Tucson"; *Crosscurrents*, "Yogurt"; *Descant*, "Talking"; *Jeopardy*, "Wordplay," "A Trick of Memory"; *Key West Review*, "The Night Nurse"; *The Laurel Review*, "The Sacred Well"; *North American Review*, "Wrestling"; *River Oak Review*, "Animal Rights"; *Santa Clara Review*, "No Answer"; *Short Story*, "Jackknife," "Men At Work"; *The Slate*, "Cross Country" (as "Some Kinds of Pain"); *South Carolina Review*, "Logjam"; *Sou'Wester*, "The New Sidewalks"; *Sundog*, "Worry," "Siding," "Skin"; *Wisconsin Fiction*, "Quick Bright Things."

"Yogurt" was reprinted in *Flash Fiction* (New York: W.W. Norton & Co., 1992). "Worry" was reprinted in *Microfiction* (New York: W.W. Norton & Co., 1996). Several short-short stories appeared in *Worry*, a chapbook published by Mark Sanders (Main-Traveled Roads, 1996).